A PENNY LANE SAGA

(Three kids from old Liverpool)

CHAPTER 1

Early Childhood near Penny Lane

Sprawling along the northern banks of the River Mersey, Liverpool, like so many other large cities during the nineteen twenties and thirties, could be a rather grim environment in which to be born and raised. Nevertheless, growing up in the city throughout this period of Liverpool's uneasy history, I and my sister managed to enjoy many very good times together despite the undoubted privations. Before and during the Great Depression years, pleasant and amusing incidents did sometimes occur to illuminate the drab monotony and very real hardships endured throughout those dark days. It wasn't all doom and gloom.

After 1900, a few years before World War I, my father served his apprenticeship as a joiner in a local Liverpool firm and, being proficient in his trade and a strong union man, he constantly endeavoured to secure, with union help, better rights and conditions of service for his friends and fellow workers during a very difficult period. Much unemployment made it hard sometimes to negotiate for improvements. During the twenties, despite competence, a tradesman could receive just one hours notice from work - if trade was slack - and be out on the street again trudging round in the soul destroying search for another job; so very often unobtainable.

However, although job prospects were fairly bleak in 1921, my father, with some degree of luck, did secure work at a large firm which seemed to offer a moderate possibility of permanency. Now, with a little fresh optimism, he discarded the, seemingly, pointless exercise of waiting for better times and nervously proposed to Beatrice, our mother to be. Working from home as a dressmaker, for very little money, she must have been delighted to receive and accept my Dad's offer of marriage, after their short but very happy courtship.

Both intelligent and shrewd, they realised that the way ahead wouldn't be at all easy. The princely joiner's wage of about two pounds a week, plus their own optimistic desire to create a successful marriage, was really the very best they could hope for in the foreseeable future. With very little money saved - about twenty pounds - they married and were able to rent, for a few shillings a week, the home where I and my sister Kate were born and spent our early years.

Not a stone's throw from Penny Lane (made famous, years later, by the musical talents of the Beatles) in the small front bedroom of a 'three-up - three-down' terrace house, I first saw the light of day during the late summer of 1923.

Sister Kate came two years later; born into that strange, uncertain world of respectable poverty.

From day one, even before we arrived, it must have been a 'hand-to-mouth' existence for our struggling parents as they tried to fashion a home from just a house. Having decorated with low cost materials and laid cheap lino on the floors, they partly furnished the home with second-hand household necessities and several items of furniture my father made, including a good bookcase which housed many of his precious books: collected over the years.

Shortage of money and the, ever present, threat of insecurity must have loomed large in their first two years of marriage and my birth must have strained their meagre resources to the limit! My dear old gran - bless her heart - 'chipped in with a few bob' from her life savings (so I was later told) when things got really difficult for Ma and Pa. How she ever managed that I'll never know, because our grandparents old age pension totalled the large sum of one pound a week! Insufficient to keep anyone above the bread line.

With very few toys to keep us happy, Kate and I, as toddlers, often used to gaze through the clean, neatly curtained front bedroom window and down a short street opposite (set at right angles to our dead straight block of terrace houses) to the main line railway where huge steam trains, with billowing grey smoke and shrieking whistles, rattled their way noisily towards Lime Street Station or, perhaps, travelling the other way to London. (The end of the world, to us kids.) We loved to watch these awe inspiring monsters occasionally whizzing past in all their majestic glory, but were happy to see them far enough away to lessen the noise that might disturb our night-time slumbers!

With little lad's enthusiasm, I proudly informed an enthralled sister, Kate, that I'd be an engine driver when I grew up! " Will you, Bernie? " she said, her big blue eyes wide with admiration, "Oh, Bernie, that'd be luvly. Will y'take me on the big puffa?" she questioned.

"Oh, yes, course, but you'll have t'go in the carriage," I replied, emphatically, "they wouldn't let girls ride on the engine!" "S'pose not!" she pouted, thoughtfully, "but y'will take me, won't y'Bernie?" "Yes, promise, "I murmured, hugging her ever so close to me.

Train spotting, with other lads from the street, became an absolute mania as we grew older and every opportunity was taken to scramble over the low wall on to Penny Lane hill embankment where, with notebooks at the ready, we'd sit for hours taking down engine numbers as the giants, vibrating the ground, thundered past and some of the drivers smiled and waved to us - that was great. Even tom-boy Kate soon joined us in our harmless pastime and noted, with glee, the many celebrities of the iron road! Simple amusements like this, which didn't cost money, were all we kids really had early on in our lives.

Top-and-whip, skipping rope and 'hopscotch' were favourite pastimes for some little girls in our street, while one or two rich kids proudly paraded dolls in fancy prams along the pavements or cavorted about in pretty dresses, trying to put less fortunate girls to shame. Yes, even kids can be snobs! Poor little Kate did have a pretty dress but her best one was kept for Sundays! She had a doll too but no pram and many's the time she played happily, in our lobby, with her little friend, Joyce, who sat another doll near to Kate's for a special pretend tea party!

Tiny dolls cups, saucers and plates were carefully laid out on a cardboard box, used as a table, while young Kate played hostess! Both children were clean, the dolls were rather 'tatty' and so was the tea set but, to the small girls, the dolls were queens, the lobby a palace and the kids enjoyed themselves in a make-believe world of their own. Poor they might be, but soon learnt to conjure happiness out of thin air! Many youngsters did: with few personal possessions they had to pretend.

We lads played 'conkers' (in season) and ' YO-YO ' was a great craze; that round, three inch, completely lethal_bobbin affair on a string which so often 'clobbered' innocent, unsuspecting passers by - including me. Marbles, played with multi-coloured glass alleys on pavements and in street gutters, was a game which sometimes caused a fracas when some 'smart alec' tried to swipe a 'brany' (brand new alley!) by making a crafty switch! Everything - even a simple YO-YO - cost money and so, with pocket money in short supply or non-existent, children usually bought very little, except a few sweets now and then!

On the whole, school days weren't so bad. However, not being particularly brilliant, Kate and I seldom relished seeing or, more importantly, ma and Pa seeing the contents of the periodic school report! 'Average' or 'Could do better' were comments we hoped wouldn't appear but they sometimes did! Learning - or should I say forcibly injected with the usual subjects, we were only truly interested in one or two. General science and drawing never bored us and Kate loved biology. Composition, writing essays, somehow appealed to me. My very strange tales must have been a constant source of great amusement to the school staff! In essays concerning our school holidays, my more than honest accounts, with graphic detail of our antics during holiday breaks, undoubtedly brought many a smile to the lips of the lady teacher - and her colleagues - because she always gave me good marks for my blotted scribble and strange pictures! She, like me, I guess, had a rather warped sense of humour!

As early school classes were mixed, boys and girls sharing the same lessons, I soon developed a lasting friendship with a good looking, though tom-boyish girl, Christine, who was ever ready with a ruler, fist or other deadly weapon, to spring to my defence when I drifted into the odd fight! Little angels we certainly weren't. Kate, a little more angelic than I, soon learned to take care of herself, under the helpful guidance of my mother-hen pal, Christine. They became really good friends and Chris, with uncanny insight, taught young Kate all she needed to know about self-preservation in a hard world!

Although most of us walked to school, a few children did travel on the old tramcar - and old they certainly were. Double decker bone shakers open to the elements at either end, with a spiral staircase leading to the top deck. Standing at the controls, the poor old driver with no cover, save a waterproof black cape which flapped about relentlessly in the wind and barely protected him from pelting rain on a cold wet day, must have been frozen to the core! With break-neck speed, the trams used to hurtle down Smithdown Road hill, from Lodge Lane, as the driver frantically clanged a warning bell, on the open platform, with a quivering half frozen foot!

At hand height, in front of the driver, a small pointed lever controlled the car mechanism, while a very large hand operated crank and foot-adjusted ratchet applied and held the

TOXTETH PARK CEMETERY
MOTHER O' GOD!
SMITHDOWN ROAD.
HELLS BELLS! MISSUS!
AH-UMMA! -THIS IS THE PENNY LANE 'FLYER!'
PENNY LANE PIER HEAD
5 Crawford's Cream Crackers
215
PENNY LANE - LODGE LANE - PIER HEAD.
VAN HOUTEN'S COCOA
LIVERPOOL CORPORATION TRAMWAYS
CLANG
BLOODY 'ELL!
GOOD GOD!
BLIMEY - FRED! GET A 'BOX' READY!
FUNERALS UNDERTAKER
OLD TRAM (BONE-SHAKER) 'HURTLING' DOWN SMITHDOWN ROAD.
1930.

brakes, when the whole rattling contraption shuddered to a grinding halt; often with loudly protesting metal wheels screeching along the steel tram-track.

Tram travel was second nature to Liverpudlians, but the apparent lack of adequate shock absorption and the hard, uncomfortable slatted seats would make modern travellers 'cringe!' Subsequent leather seated, improved chassis trams gave a far more comfortable, less nerve shattering and warmer ride. The modern, all enclosed, cream and green tram - the so called Green Goddess - appearing on Liverpool streets in the late thirties, was a very great improvement on the old bone shakers. It was an absolute 'nine-days-wonder' and we, as kids in our untidy jackets, caps and half mast socks, stopped in our tracks to gaze, fascinated, at the sleek lines and sparkling glossy paint work of our brand new 'up-to-the-minute' vehicles.

We, as a family, walked nearly everywhere except, perhaps, for the odd trip to town when the 'sales' were on at Lewis's, Blacklers or Church Street 'Woolies' (Woolworth 3d and 6d store - nothing over three pence or six pence, old money; when the shop really did belong to Woolworths)

Low family funds meant that we children often saw lovely things we'd like but could never hope to own. Seeing so-called rich kids with little bikes, we both longed for one the same but knew the thought was just another day dream - like winning a competition prize. Then, one Saturday, 'out-of-the-blue' it happened! With a big smile on his face. Dad came into the kitchen and called Kate and me out into the old back yard. There, leaning against the coal shed wall, was a small 'fairy-cycle.' Second-hand, just a one-piece tubular frame with handlebars, brakes, pedals and solid tyred wheels, it was the simplest cycle ever seen. BUT - it was a GLORIOUS BIKE! To Kate and me it was like a bag of gold.

Quickly opening the back door, with frantic excitement, we giggled and jostled one another for the 'first go' on the little bike!."Go on, Kate, you go first." I conceded gallantly, secretly thinking, no doubt, that she'd fall off first. Grinning nervously, she struggled to position her tiny "bum" on the saddle while Pa steadied the handlebars. Slowly wobbling down the middle of our back entry, young Kate kept her small legs wide to scoot, rather than peddle, craftily saving herself from falling off! My big brother show off tactics, trying hard to pedal, proved to be a comical disaster, a comedy of errors which lead to my falling off, of course. Kate didn't laugh and ran to help me up; a kind action which did nothing for my manly image. Despite my scraped bare knees and aching back and Kate's wobble into the wall, we practised all afternoon, with pa's help, and soon more or less 'got-the-hang-of-it' - as kids usually do. At least, we had a bike and, after those few hair raising antics up and down the 'jigger,' we were hardly ever off that great little bike.

In the following weeks, standing on our front door step. Pa had many a hearty laugh watching that strange and comical velocipede belting along the pavements with our Kate straddled across the squeaky seat, while I bobbed up and down like mad in front, standing on the pedals, cycling like the 'clappers.' That trusty cycle (bought for the princely sum of 7/6 - 37p - from a pal whose daughter had outgrown it) really got a pounding over the next few years. What those solid tyred wheels did to our poor 'bums' isn't hard to imagine.

One warm and sunny afternoon, shortly after the very happy bike event, Kate and I witnessed the quite most extraordinary sight of our lifetime. As friends and neighbours chatted by their front doors and we kids played in the street, a sudden excited shout attracted everyone's attention and we all gazed aloft to where a man was pointing; a look of complete surprise and incredulity on his face. Way above the roof tops - over Penny Lane hill - very slowly drifting towards us, was a huge, incredible, oval silver balloon. Clearly visible, on the front end of this airborne miracle, were the very large characters - R-100! Brilliant sunshine glinted on the shiny surface of the massive dirigible as it glided silently over our street and moved,

R100 GLIDES OVER PENNY LANE HILL AND ALVERSTONE ROAD — MID-1930.

with stately dignity, across the main line railway and, as with fascination we watched it growing ever smaller, slowly disappeared into the bright, clear blue sky.

Last of the large airships, built for public transport, this curious and magnificent craft's image always lingers in our memories. It was the first and last time that we ever saw such a strange and, to us, fantastic sight! Disaster, which overtook the R-101, brought the British airship industry to an abrupt halt. In the early hours of the morning of October 5th 1930, the ill-fated airship struck a low hill near Beauvais, in France, and was consumed by fire in minutes, with the loss of 47 lives. This horror resulted in the immediate grounding of the R-100 (seen by us over Penny Lane) and very soon after that the memorable craft was broken up for scrap. The catastrophic end of the German airship Hindenburg, which burst into flames at Lakehurst, America, in 1937, really put an end to this form of travel. As hydrogen (potentially explosive) gas was used to fill the gasbags inside the envelope of these extraordinary craft, it seems a blessing that any further construction and use was finally abandoned. Helium, being inert and very light, might have been used but is, perhaps, more expensive. You tell me! I'm not an economist or even an aircraft builder.

Very noticeable at this period in our lives and well remembered, was the comparative absence of street crime and the very much more friendly and caring attitudes of neighbours, acquaintances and even strangers. There were exceptions to the rule - there always are - but, by and large, mutual trust and respect were observed in daily life and neighbourly help was always available in a crisis - if at all possible - during some very difficult times. Front doors often left open (for children to run in and out) never ever posed the threat of anyone being robbed or seriously attacked in their own home. Frequently, we children happily wandered down to Greenbank or Sefton Park to play with little or no fear of being pestered or molested, in any way, by mindless, evil perverts.

Neat and tidy, with well washed, donkey stoned front steps and brightened red or yellow sandstone cills, our little terraced houses were always equally 'spick and span' inside - as kids playing would allow - but behind the sparkling windows and clean net curtains, tell tale traces of poverty were hard to conceal in very many local homes. While a small minority of folks living in the street, with reasonably secure jobs, were looked upon as being well off, their lifestyles were simple and very mediocre compared to modern standards,

For our parents, leisure time was scarce. Pa, when he wasn't at work, made improvements to the house or constructed furniture or other items to make our lives more comfortable and pleasant. The large kitchen table, a handy adjustable easy chair and a very nice bookcase, were articles he fashioned from second-hand wood, using his expert skill as a good joiner.

Domestic refrigerators weren't available to us and so dad made a very useful wooden meatsafe with perforated zinc panelled sides which, being fitted in the cold, airy back yard, really kept our perishable food nice and fresh for quite a time. Except for ceilings, which Pa usually tackled first with a whitewash brush, Mam, between her many household chores, became quite proficient at interior decoration. Probably unlike kids today, Kate and I enjoyed helping with the work. Fetching wallpaper, holding the step-ladder or trotting in and out with buckets of paste or whitewash, was a great game to us. Our occasional fooling about - daubing each other with left overs from the buckets - brought forth sharp words from Ma and Pa, smirking broadly, tried to keep a straight face. Always seeing the funny side, he seldom intervened, (much to Ma's annoyance) " You just encourage the kids to play the fool," she'd say sternly. Pa would slip us a sly wink, " Just behave y'selves, you two, or I'll come down and give y'one!" he'd shout severely. He rarely smacked us, though; little devils that we were. They were really great, the pair of them.

After the 1926 General Strike, when unemployment was rife over the whole country, Pa did manage to hold down a job for most of the time. We, I suppose, were luckier than many throughout this unhappy period when, even during 1931 - 32, due to religious unrest and appalling living conditions amongst many poor working people there were street riots in Liverpool and Birkenhead. As children, we were kept out of harm's way and didn't see anything of these troubles. A mass hunger strike, in 1932, drew very many people, from all over Britain, to a large demonstration in London and mounted police officers were used to quell riots in Hyde Park. Mounted baton charges were frequently employed, in the twenties and thirties, to subdue disorderly crowds or riots.

Trouble in Liverpool, we do both remember, bubbled up when Oswald Moseley's 'black-shirts' clashed with the communists and others whose ideologies were poles apart. Poor little Kate, then only about ten, asked me, fearfully, "Will those awful black-shirts come and take our house, Bernie?" "Erm - no, - that is no, course not. Don't be silly!" I answered with nervous reassurance! I'd seen Moseley's ranting on the cinema newsreels and I wasn't at all happy about 'black-shirts.'

One brighter spot, during this disturbed era, was the opening, by King George V in 1934, of the new Mersey Tunnel. Connecting Liverpool and Birkenhead by a great new road under the river was, to us, something fantastic. Describing it as 'A great feat of civil engineering' - the *Liverpool Echo* also proudly stated that 'It is the longest underwater tunnel in the world!' Before traffic was permitted to drive through this modern wonder, the general public were to be given the unique opportunity of walking - an approximate couple of miles - under the great River Mersey for the first time.

Being a 'nine-days-wonder' Pa agreed to take us all down to experience this once-in-a-lifetime event. Dressed in our Sunday best, Kate and I excitedly accompanied Ma and Pa along Penny Lane to catch the number 5 to town, from a stop close to the old tram sheds in Smithdown Road. In luck with the weather, we didn't have long to wait, either, for the crowded tram. Full on the lower deck, we all trundled up the spiral stairs (much to Ma's disgust) and, of course, we kids wanted to sit on the outside circular seat at the top. As three people were just alighting, we got our favourite spot at the back of the tram.

Sniffing the gloriously cold air, we heard Ma faintly murmur, " Thank heavens we're not at the front", the implication being that one got a great deal more fresh air at the front than the back! Incidentally, the only thing between one's bum and the outside world, on this seat, was an 18 inch high band of steel netting curving round at the back.

With two pulls on a cord, operating a bell on the driver's platform, the conductor's ding-ding set the car moving jerkily forward with nerve shattering effect. Past the old Grand cinema and on up Smithdown Road towards Lodge Lane, the rickety old tram took us nearby the hospital and, I might add, the cemetery. Someone with a warped sense of humour must have put the two so close together. Soon appearing at the top of the stairs, the conductor, with large leather bag of change at his waist and ticket punching machine slung from one shoulder, called cheerily, "Fares, please." Dad gave him 6d for the four of us and, with a curious pinging sound, he punched four tickets and handed them over. (That small old money fare should raise a smile).

Once beyond Lodge Lane, we were half way to town and the tram rattled on down Upper Parliament Street, passing the well known Rialto cinema, and soon reached our stop, in Church Street, where Ma needed a few things from 'Woolies'. With mother's bits and pieces stowed away in her shopping bag - no plastic bags then - we made our way, with great excitement, into Whitechapel and on towards the new Queensway area at the mouth of our great new Mersey Tunnel. Motivated by newspaper articles, many, many people had gathered for the event and now everyone converged on the imposing, and to us kids, massive entrance to this modern marvel. Highly impressed, we followed our fellow Liverpudlians, with awe and some trepidation, down the gentle slope for our first ever walk under the turbulent waters of the River Mersey. Suddenly grabbing my hand tightly, Kate, with an apprehensive look in her clear blue eyes, whispered nervously, "I'm a bit scared, Bernie - Is it safe - d'you think the water will get in?" Attempting a reassuring smile, I murmured, "No, Kate, luv, I don't think so. They wouldn't let us come down 'ere if it wasn't safe, would they?" "S'pose not" she chirped uneasily, while still tightly clasping my hand.

Crowds of curious, laughing walkers surrounding us tended to boost our confidence and we all pressed on into the tunnel as Kate, still nervous, dragged me over to Pa in order to seize his hand as well - just in case. Once inside the unbelievable structure, our apprehension slowly faded when Ma and Pa drew our attention to details of this strange new environment as we very slowly ambled down, down, down beneath the ancient river. Dark side walls rising from the maintenance walkways gave way, at about ten feet, to a brightly lit domed roof of the tunnel. Everything roads, side panels, lights and roof were clean and sparklingly new. No trace or hint of grime or oily patches showed now to mar it's pristine appearance but, very soon, all this would change as the future heavy traffic was allowed to thunder through, en route to innumerable destinations all over the country.

Striding wearily uphill, past the half way mark, everything seemed monotonously the same as we slowly reached daylight once again and Liverpool's sister port of Birkenhead. Knowing this side of the river, Pa took us to Hamilton Square gardens, in front of the Town Hall, for a promised picnic lunch. Tired after the long walk but thrilled to bits, we kids skidaddled up the nearest diagonal path of the delightfully colourful gardens and 'plonked' ourselves down on a nice wooden seat, ready for our long awaited picnic.

In this ideal spot, Ma unearthed the flask and opened up the big bag of 'goodies' she'd brought along. Tucking in, with relish, we all enjoyed the open air meal, sitting there in the warm welcome sunshine. Pa's notion of returning to Liverpool by ferry might seem, to modern children, a very tame event but to us, with very little money, it was simply marvellous to - go on the boat! Sparrows and pigeons fought for left over crumbs as we packed up and, with great delight, toddled off to Woodside Ferry for that wonderful sail across the river. Excitedly jostling through the clicking turnstiles at the ferry, where Pa paid a few coppers fare, Kate and I ran down the sloping bridge to Birkenhead landing stage, where our great little one-funnelled dream boat could be seen bobbing merrily over the choppy Mersey waters towards us.

The 'Woodchurch', I think it was, dropped its noisy gangway onto the well-worn wooden stage and Ma nervously held us back as the jostling crowds disembarked. Quickly, we ran on ahead and up the stairs to the top deck of the boat. I can still hear my Pa's voice ringing in my ears, as we noisily clambered up the iron clad stairway, "Calm down, you kids, calm down, for heaven's sake. Don't climb on the ship's rail, you'll be in the flaming river.

As the deck shuddered and noisy engines roared into life, we reached the stern and excitedly knelt up on the slatted wooden seat, peering over the guard rail at the furiously churning sea above the propellers. Our wonderful little boat was pulling away from the stage, we were on our way. Never still, with wild delight - as Pa nearly did a hornpipe - we ran along the deck, past a smoking funnel, to the bows for a glorious view of massive waves drifting away on either side, as the ship cut through the turbulent waters like a sharpened knife. Wind blew our hair straight back and Kate tried hard to smile, "Y'look like a frightened rabbit" she shouted loudly, above the gale. "So d'you, cheeky monkey," I tried to bellow back. Gleefully laughing, we sat down on a slightly sheltered seat, clinging together closely against the buffeting wind. Opposite, a windblown middle-aged lady smiled as she frantically tried to fix a large scarf over her head, to prevent a very fancy hat from being, unceremoniously, wrenched away. All three of us laughed at her final success. "Mind you don't get blown overboard". She laughingly tried to shout above the din.

Glorious sea air and tangy salt spray was something out of this world to us, and we just hated the thought of having to leave it all behind. "Come on, you two, time to go," bellowed Pa, as he caught up with us grinning at the lady who'd nearly lost her hat. "Nice kids." She called out. "As long as they're being watched," Dad laughed, cheerfully. "Come on, let's go." Catching up with Ma at the head of the stairs, we could just see the gangway being lowered. A fairly low tide made it quite a climb from Princes landing stage, up the floating bridge, to the Pier Head tram terminus. Cold but delighted, we all made it and soon got a dear old tram back home. For Kate and me, the day had been a marvellous one to remember. For children today, I suppose, with television, computers and all the rest of modern paraphernalia, our day would have meant nothing. Ah, well, that's progress, isn't it.

Weeks went by, much as usual, without any great event. School days it seems, for many like us, were best for the pranks we played and the scrapes we got ourselves into. Except for the subjects that we liked, learning was, I'm sorry to say, of secondary consideration in our naughty little lives.

A certain unfortunate lady, Miss Keating, our sometimes, chemistry teacher (christened by us bug powder, for obvious reasons) was tall and thin with a mop of red hair and looked much like a Bunsen burner - lit. We, little devils, tormented her rotten with comically stupid answers to questions, which greatly amused other kids. Sometimes we made hidden references to her physical appearance; knowing full well that everyone understood - except the dear lady herself. I'm sure she did, but she didn't 'crack on.' Children, at times, can be very sarcastic and unwittingly cruel.

Another quite pleasant, round-faced and very full bosomed, lady teacher was, I'm afraid, the subject of a great deal of our misplaced amusement. Wearing a highly coloured floral smock, she, her eyebrows, hands and smock always became covered in chalk dust as her hand, clutching a chalk or eraser, flew deftly across the blackboard. Presenting a highly comical spectacle, she faced the class like a very busy bakery worker. Apart from this obvious cause for hilarity amongst the kids, the dear lady, when provoked, had a habit of agitating cruising up and down the narrow aisle between the desks, like a colourful sloop in full sail, with outstretched arm and very chalky finger bobbing about, trying to quell a minor disruption in class. Face red as a turkey cock, while muttering incoherent remarks and with a strangely comical glint in her eye, she attempted to convey her displeasure and the immediate need for a bit more order and decorum. It never worked and we kids found it hard to conceal our wicked mirth. Sometimes this unfortunate female stood - laying down the law - alongside a front desk at which sat a tall, thin wicked lad (incongruous because of his height) who caused much merriment by pretending to bore a hole, with his finger, in the ample bosom of the poor teacher, when she wasn't looking. I think she knew he was up to something, but could never catch him at it. The same lad was often responsible for other misdemeanours, too numerous to mention.

The occasional small glass 'stink bomb,' strategically placed under the teacher's desk; calcium carbide in the ink-wells or inked blotting paper pellets flicked about, with deadly effect, with the help of short wooden rulers, were some of the many relatively harmless tricks we played and for which we, sometimes, got caught. When, one day, my own ink-well started bubbling like Vesuvius during class - to the great annoyance of the female teacher - I protested, "Please miss, it wasn't me - honest." Realising, with dodgy logic, that I was unlikely to drop carbide in my own ink-well, she believed me and sought the true culprit! What she didn't know, however, was the fact that it was I who obtained most of the carbide, used for 'nefarious practices,' in the first place. Happy Days.

Young Christine, mentioned earlier, occupied a desk in front of mine during lessons and, always ready for a laugh, she dropped a foot rule beneath her own desk and, having bent down to pick it up, pushed it, with great expertise, under my desk and right up the leg of my shorts. Having leapt about two feet in the air, I tried to explain to a bemused teacher that I'd got cramp in my leg; adding under my breath to Chris that I'd get her at break time. A great deal of giggling by those near enough to see the caper didn't improve the teacher's temper, as can be imagined, and she gave us all the length of her tongue, adding that the class needed to pay much more attention to hard work.

Tomboy that she was, Chris still wanted me to notice and treat her like a girl. Her plans seemed to work for, having chased her round the school yard a couple of times - as threatened - and cornering her near the bike shed, I managed, after a lot of slap and tickle, to win my first real kiss. I was just eleven; she was a grown up twelve!

Fairly healthy, except for the odd cold now and then, I suddenly, one day, came home from school feeling really ill with a feverish condition and very sore throat. Thinking that I'd picked up tonsilitis, Ma kept me home and away from our Kate. As the illness seemed to worsen, she sent for the doctor - usually a last resort because of the expense. After examination and very painful throat swabs, I was put to bed without protest because I felt so poorly. Next day, made to gargle with an odd liquid after coughing up mucous, I was given an injection and subsequently knew very little of the hectic activity going on in the rest of the house.

Seeing no one for the next few days, except Ma dressed in a long white coat and with her nose and mouth suitably covered, I was almost too ill to notice that she'd placed a strange little oil lamp on the dressing table; a weird contraption supporting a container of fluid (apparently called 'Cresolene') on the top. This Aladdin's lamp, with it's peculiar vaporizing liquid, emitted pungent fumes intended to fumigate the room and prevent infection spreading to those in attendance. Whether or not this medical marvel was of any use, I'm not really sure!

Unbeknown to me, young Kate had been packed off to our aunt's house, a couple of streets away. Outside my bedroom door, a large disinfectant impregnated sheet was fixed and no one, but Ma and the doctor, was allowed to enter the room. Given nothing to eat but milk and white of egg, which I could hardly swallow, and deprived of any company, I felt extremely unhappy and terribly isolated, to say the least. And, of course, isolated I just had to be.

"Where's Pa and Kate?" I asked, after what seemed an eternity. "Oh, your dad's had to do some work away - he - he'll be back in a few days." Mother murmured, rather unconvincingly. Somehow I knew that it wasn't true but I was too weak and poorly to argue. "Kate's here, isn't she? I whispered faintly, quietly sobbing, "Well, y'see, luv," Ma said softly, tears filling her kind grey eyes, "we don't want her to catch any nasty germs, do we? She'll be up to see you in a few days when you're a bit better, luv". " Will it be very long, Mam?" I pleaded, tearfully?" Desperately trying to choke back the tears, she answered, brokenly, "No, no, it won't be - it won't be very long now, luv."

A second anti-toxin serum injection, given by the doctor, hardly made me stir: I was so ill. It seemed, too, that the ever present peculiar odour emanating from Aladdin's lamp lulled me into a strange, disturbed uneasy sleep. How many days passed I'm not sure, but one morning I woke up to less pain and thought that I might be getting better. Vaguely, I remember Ma being with me most of the time and the fact that the side bedroom window was slightly open - day and night - although a small coal fire burned brightly in a little old iron grate! Weak as a kitten, I was only allowed out of bed a little at a time until my strength returned, which took several weeks. One day, while looking through the window, watching the kids playing in the street, I suddenly heard the bedroom door open and in walked Pa! "Pa! Pa! " I cried, nearly falling over as I turned towards him.

Tears filled my eyes, "Oh, Pa!" I sobbed, "where've you been - where've you been?" His comforting arms encircled my quivering body and he hugged me tightly, as never before. For a while he couldn't speak and then he said, hesitantly, "Son, son, you've been very poorly, they'd only let your mum in here 'til now." "But why, Pa?" I cried, "T'was only that 'what's it,' that tonsil thing, wasn't it?" Silent again for a moment, his eyes filled as he looked down at me and whispered, "No, Son, no, you've had a real bad do this time; you've had diphtheria pretty bad. Thought we might lose you, Son." Tears streamed down his cheeks. I'd never ever seen my Pa cry before. "Oh God son. Your Ma and I thought we'd lose you." He cried and hugged me ever more closely to him. We both cried a lot, I'm not ashamed to say.

Later that same week, I came downstairs and a couple of days afterwards, we all had to evacuate the place while two burly men from the local health authority came with special gear to fumigate the whole house. Although my health did improve, I was left with a damaged heart muscle, from the diphtheria toxins, and had to take it easy for a very long time.

Not so very long after my illness, poor, dear Kate became sick with watery eyes and sneezing, at first thought to be a cold which, as the tell-tale rash appeared on her little face and neck, turned out to be a very unpleasant, but mild, attack of childhood measles. With a 'near fatal' malady just behind me, it was no real surprise when I was sent off to my aunt's house, as Kate had been during my serious illness. Poorly for two or three weeks, Kate, tough little girl that she was, quickly made a full recovery. Out of harm's way, I dodged the extremely unpleasant germ which plagued so very many youngsters at that time.

Looking back, I know that those two enforced separations, when young, brought Kate and me much closer together from then on. Death, to a child, is very frightening and we both knew that I'd been quite close to it. Our cousin had already died of post-diphtheria. Time apart, in those alarming circumstances, created in us a deep concern for each other's welfare and formed a fresh bond between us. That bond has greatly strengthened over the years.

Meals were adequate in our young days; nothing fancy, but we never starved. A chip shop at the top of Penny Lane hill did a roaring trade, I remember, not only in family meals but in many odd pen'orths, in small paper bags, bought by us youngsters when we had the cash. Gathering round the 'chippy,' for something to do and somewhere to go, we'd sit on the large wooden shop window cill or even an old coat on the pavement and chat, tease or generally fool about. Lots of bags and very greasy chip paper drifted around, I'm afraid, much to the annoyance of nearby shop keepers.

Sweets to tempt children, displayed in a wondrous shop window lower down the hill, made our young mouths water when we hadn't got the money to buy them. Anything from dolly mixtures, three corner packet sherbet dabs complete with lolly and licorice stick, innumerable sugar dolls, animals and sticky toffees plus very sickly sweet pink sugar creams, small, thin wooden boxes filled with sherbet cotaining also, a tin spoon (a positive health hazard) which now makes me shudder and really puts my teeth on edge. A penny or tu'pence a quarter was the price of most sweets, toffees and chocolates.

KATE AND ME EN-ROUTE TO PENNY LANE 'CHIPPY' 1935

Four pence was dear and six pence a quarter sweets were in screw top bottles on the top shelf only for the rich and famous. For special occasions, Cadburys sold milk tray chocolates, available in small dark blue, gold lettered boxes, for six pence a quarter and about a shilling for half a pound. Five new pence, today. Years later, Kate and I often laughed about those unbelievable prices which, at the time, we just couldn't afford.

Christmas inevitably came round and we always managed to enjoy a good plain dinner with chicken or a duck, roast potatoes and a vegetable, followed by a home made Christmas pudding, Christmas presents were always very simple. Usually we received some fruit, a few sweets and, perhaps, a tin toy for me and a doll or cheap game for Kate. These small gifts were really the most we could hope for. Strange as it may seem, we were happy because we knew, in our hearts, that Ma and Pa did their level best with the bit they had. Christmas crackers were on the table over the holiday and streamers, tinsel, silver stars and paper chains came out of last years box for Pa, bless his heart, to decorate the room like a Christmas grotto. We all had paper hats and little decorations on our clothes.

Happily, it wasn't just the material things we had, over those few days, which really mattered to us, but something that has, sadly, disappeared from many homes today, a close family bond, a feeling of 'togetherness' so very precious to our small family of four. Everyone is different, of course, but Christmas now seems so, commercialized. Children are brain-washed to want the earth, everyone in fact, wants the earth. No-one ever appears to be satisfied. So very much is now available on credit, which seems to be a very mixed blessing. There always comes the day of reckoning for which so many folks, who've taken credit, are very often ill prepared. (No-one, in this life, ever gets a free breakfast.) Our parents never ran into debt; I think that they were right.

Expensive gifts, apparently, don't always bring happiness in their wake, either. Lots of people so easily become bored with presents received and almost go berserk if something new isn't readily available. We were born poor and learned to appreciate and value our material possessions much more and didn't discard them without good reason. While realising the need for better articles to improve our lives, we didn't regard such things as indispensable. Sophistication, I'm afraid, was a thing that we had yet to learn. (Sorry for the digression, dear reader; I'll try and press on.)

Just before our teens, my high spirited young friend, Christine, had been moved to an all girls school and so had Kate. Frequently out and about with a lad of my own age, I might have lost touch with Chris but for the fact that she and Kate remained friendly, although in different classes at school. Young Chris often visited our house, ostensibly to see Kate but, I was soon to learn, young ladies can be very devious in the nicest possible way when they have romance on their mind.

Knowing when I wasn't going out with my mate, young sister Kate would persuade me to accompany her and Chris to the 'flicks' (the cinema) or even for a walk to Sefton Park palm house, Calderstones Park or where ever, if we'd run short of cash. What the pair were up to dawned on me one day when Kate, saying that she wasn't well, wanted Chris and me to visit the cinema alone. Observing, with some amusement, my expression of awkward surprise, they couldn't keep straight faces and burst out laughing.

Chris, grabbing my arm, giggled, "What's up, darling, where's the problem? Am I that bad looking, dearie?" Unusually, I blushed because, although I'd known Chris for so long as a pal, it was only now that I realised a much deeper feeling was stirring within me for the pretty, scheming little minx.

Although we saw the romantic film at the Grand cinema (alone - as planned), some bits of the story were missed, I'm afraid, because we happened to be sitting on the back row of the stalls and - well, we were only about fourteen; it was warm, semi-dark and very romantic. This innocent little episode of childhood sticks in both our minds for two very good reasons firstly, it was really the beginning of our courtship and secondly, it happened to be Coronation year of 1937, a time of national celebration. This period of glitter and pageantry, which won the hearts and minds of many in Liverpool and everywhere in the country, was the first opportunity we'd had to witness a coronation. Amidst attendant pomp and ceremony, the Prince was crowned King George VI and his Queen, Elizabeth, was destined to become the beloved Queen Mother at the end of the twentieth century.

Jubilee year of 1935 had been a public high spot of the thirties, but the impressive, spectacular and world acclaimed crowning of a new King and Queen, after the strange abdication of Edward VIII, a year earlier, was something which really served to brighten the spirits of everyone in Britain, (if not their economic situation) During an otherwise dismal decade. Enthusiasm for the event was increased by the fact that much of it was broadcast on the 'wireless' and also on this 'new fangled' thing called 'television'. (In the London area only).

Hearing only the wireless version of the great occasion, we were thrilled and excited listening to the graphic description of this extraordinary spectacle, including the journey to and from Westminster Abbey by the Royal Cortege. Visiting the Grand cinema, later in the week, we enjoyed actually seeing the magnificent and fascinating pageant on film. A pre-television spectacular, we'd always remember. Street parties were held all over Liverpool. 'End-to-end tables laden with tasty foods (miraculously appearing out of thin air), fancy ribbons, bunting and emblems of the new King and Queen, enhanced the festivities and served to brighten the otherwise drab streets. Life, it seemed at this time, was improving for some of us, but we couldn't yet see the darkened clouds gathering on the horizon. The very troubled years ahead. It was just as well that we remained in blissful ignorance of the future, for those two short years from 1937 to 39 were quite happy for us as a family; the best we would enjoy of many yet to come.

Looking back to the twenties and early thirties, I realise that we must have been 'well off compared to many others living in Liverpool during those lean years. Our little terrace house wasn't bad. It only had gas lighting, coal burning fires and an old iron kitchen range, but our Ma kept the place 'spick-and-span', reasonably well furnished (on the money she got) and made the house into a great little home. Lack of an inside toilet (only a loo' down the yard) was something we were used to, at that time. Mother was a good manager (she had to be) and an excellent needle-woman, but how she fed and clothed us all, I'll never know. Not only did she repair garments, but made them larger, at times, even for our dad. He mended our shoes, before hard wear really ruined them, with the expertise of a professional cobbler.

Thanks to industrious parents therefore, we had reasonably good shoes and clothing during those hard times, when so many other kids didn't. A vivid reminder of this simple fact occurred to me when I was only about six years old. This brief 'flash back takes us to a time when my grandma lived near Princes Road (on the way to town). Often, when walking through Sefton Park and the many streets beyond to Gran's house, we'd sometimes see children poorly clothed, running about in bare feet. The apparently trivial incident, which lingers in my mind, took place outside an old pub at the corner of Berkley Street. Clinging very tightly to Ma's arm, as she wheeled Kate's rickety go-chair quickly down the street, I noticed three very large black men arguing loudly outside the pub, while a couple more scruffy looking individuals leaned against the railings of a nearby house. As a child, black people - really black with big white eyes - scared me to death. Hardly had I recovered from the shock of our brief encounter with the 'black trio,' when several lads, of differing ages, shot out of Stanhope Street across our path and on up the street, shouting and swearing, loudly. One lad, about my age, had ragged short pants with a large tear at the back through which showed his little 'bum.' His bare feet were filthy, as were the feet and legs of those lads with him.

Kate's push chair wheels squeaked a bit as Ma, hurrying on towards Princes Boulevard, dragged me along behind her - still endeavouring to look back at the cursing scruffy lads. "Ma, Ma - why're those lads like that?" I managed to say, breathlessly. "Why've they all got bare feet and dirty clothes?" By the chemist, on the corner of Princes Road, Ma stopped wheeling the push chair and looked down at me. Wiping her eyes and nose with a hanky, she whispered, "Cold today, son, makes your nose run, doesn't it?" "Those boys, mum," I persisted, "why're they like that?" Ma stood quite still, looking down at me and wiped her eyes again. Silent for a moment, she then said, quietly, "They're very poor, Bernie, they haven't got shoes and things , that's what happens when you're poor. We're very lucky, Bernie, try to remember that." Again Ma dabbed her eyes as she noticed little Kate, open mouthed, silent and scared, looking up at us from the push chair. In those few brief moments, on the street corner, I think that Ma was desperately wondering about us - about all the things she had to do, to cope with, to find a way out of our difficult situation our own little poverty trap. She prayed, no doubt, that times would improve to make it possible for us to enjoy a happier adult life, free from the many frightening money worries she had to face.

Recollections of that early childhood memory and the ever present evidence of deprivation, so noticeable in the town as we grew up, made Kate and me much more appreciative of the clothes and possessions we had and very conscious of the need for saving and thrift. Life for the family, during the next decade, might be a struggle but we knew that we'd survive. All 'tryers' and good workers, we could adapt and make the best of things and above all, like all Liverpudlians, we had a sense of humour. People of Liverpool have a tremendous flair for comedy and mirth probably because adversity is often the mother of humour. Without sometimes seeing the funny side of things, when times were hard, I think that Liverpudlians would have long since given up the ghost. Whilst ready to take a joke against ourselves, we like to 'pull other people's legs' and can always recognise humour and comedy in the most unlikely situations and the strangest places.

That's why so many good comics hail from the Liverpool area! For us as youngsters, leisure time entertainment was fairly simple and although change was on the way, it could still be some way ahead. Electrical technology was only slowly developing and, except for simple wireless and the newly evolving cinema pictures, sophisticated amusements weren't available. Dancing, a current craze with many young people, didn't appeal to us and theatres were a bit expensive.

Having so often seen the trouble caused by drunken behaviour, Pa - almost teetotal -frightened us away from alcohol. I think that he might have been right. Pleasure derived from the second-hand 'wind up' gramophone was rather short lived because one had to buy records. (Steel needles, too, on the 78 r.p.m records caused rapid wear and 'scratchy' reproduction.)

Early wireless, starting with the 2LO station in 1922, was really a very welcome source of relatively cheap entertainment for 'the masses'. Cheap, that is, if one could build a receiver similar to the one Dad made. Firstly a 'dead easy' crystal detector set and then a more elaborate valve wireless (made with the help of magazine diagrams). Buying major parts and making the rest, Pa assembled the whole Heath Robinson affair on a large wooden board. An attached Bakelite strip supported the controls. The small rechargeable 'wet battery' (lighting the valves) and a large 'dry battery' (high tension) for the power, completed the weird contraption, and it worked. Dad, handier than most, constructed sets for others, (if they bought the parts) much to Ma's annoyance, at times. Mind you, as a rule, he made a 'bob' or two on the deal.

Today, the thirties seem dreadful. Well, in some ways they were but, as the old cliché says, 'What you never have, you never miss'. And because we didn't have a lot, of anything, but made the best of what we did have, we very often really enjoyed life, despite all the miseries and drawbacks. Curiously enough, too, it didn't seem quite so bad then as it does now, looking back! Folks own or seek to own so very much now, don't they? Unlike today, people didn't waste anything; throw things away 'at the drop of a hat.' We hoarded odds and ends and made use of anything and everything. Our early teaching of thrift and careful management payed off and made a deal of difference to our lives during and after the War of 1939 - 45.

However, before the war clouds gathered and, as Pa would say, put the 'flaming 'kybosh' on everything for five long years, Kate, I and the families enjoyed what we could. Very bad winters plagued us from time to time, but in spring and summer we always made the most of any good weather. By our early teens, Kate, Chris and I had, by selling 'this and that,' bought second hand bikes. When not at school or helping in the house, *The Three Musketeers* - as they called us - cycled off into the glorious country. It was great to get away from the town for just a day! Until we got our 'cycling legs', we'd just go to Gateacre, Cronton or Tarbock (places with green fields and trees at that time). More ambitious runs soon followed and then we often crossed the Mersey and made our way, with youthful excitement, to 'Welsh' Wales.

Enjoying the bracing sail by normal ferry, we sometimes used the little remembered luggage boat' (a large open decked ship with very small bridge and funnel set in the middle). These strange little boats carried everything from cattle, cars, vans, horses with carts to our small bikes and many other 'odds and ends' which people needed to transport.

A 'floating' road-bridge (part metal strips, part wooden sets) from Georges Dock gates to the half mile long Princes Landing Stage, could be a steep and 'tricky' short journey for three little bikes if the tide happened to be low. Being young and crazy, we usually had a go; sometimes with near disastrous results.

Rock Ferry, nearer to the Welsh road, was our favoured landing spot but we used Birkenhead Woodside, if our usual boat wasn't in. On warm, sunny summer days, once we'd reached the Welsh road and past Ledsham and Queensferry, our sturdy young legs would pedal protesting iron steeds along the coast road towards Flint, Mostyn and on to Prestatyn. Time, and our legs, permiting, we sometimes made it to Colwyn Bay but that was a bit much and knees trembled by the time we reached home, late at night! Wherever we landed, be it grassy slope or sandy beach, out came the picnic lunches always tucked away in our haversacks. Bread and scrape sarnies if we had some filling, bit of chocolate, bottles of water with lemonade powder and an orange or apple. This was the outdoor banquet for the Three Musketeers. But they enjoyed every scrap in the glorious Welsh air.

With the beach always a possibility, the girls wore swim suits under their clothes and I had trunks under mine. Paddling near the shore was our usual delight, allowing a quick dry-off to return home. Fooling about in the water did get our 'cossies' a bit wet and we had to dry out, lying in the sun. After one particularly hectic half hour in the sea at Colwyn Bay, I strolled slowly up the beach and sat down on the warm sand. Rubbing my back with a small towel, idly watching the two girls still in the water, I saw Kate wave and then Chris turned, waving madly with both hands high above her head. Laughing and splashing about, the pair of them were very soon 'gingerly' picking their way up the pebble strewn shore towards me. For the first time, as they approached, Chris's rapidly developing figure aroused in me feelings which my mind tried to kid me I just hadn't got.

From a gawky school girl; all legs and eyes, Chris was quickly becoming a very desirable young woman. Nearly three years younger, Kate was still quite girlish. As my kid sister and Chris sat down, either side of me, I felt extremely warm and it wasn't just the sun.

Gazing at Chris for several moments, deep in fantasy, I suddenly muttered something quite inane about the landscape, in order to quell my erotic dream and drag my mind back to reality. (Being the thirties, young lads sexy thoughts weren't supposed to surface). "Yes, it's luvly 'ere, isn't it?" Kate said, looking at me curiously, sensing the oddness of my remarks. Pebbles jiggled and rattled noisily as the incoming tide chased them up the beach towards us. "Oh, gosh, it's really great 'ere, by the sea. I'd love to stay 'ere, wouldn't you?" Exclaimed Chris, "By heck, you've caught the sun, Bernie," she cried, "D'you feel alright, you're red all over?"

"Yes, yes, I'm fine, bit tired. It's a heck of a long run, that. We'd better rest a bit ready for the long 'jag' home." I answered, nervously. I really was tired and lazily lay back sideways, with one elbow supporting myself on the sand. Suddenly, Chris leaned over and, with that wicked look in her eyes, whispered, "You're lazy, that's your trouble, chucks." Giggling, she made as if to push my supporting elbow, resting on the shore. I grabbed her wrist and, of course, with great precision, she fell across my bare chest her sensuous body pressed so closely to me and her lovely face so very close to mine.

In a flash, my eager arms were tightly round her as I passionately kissed those warm, inviting red lips. My heart pounded; my senses reeled, I almost felt as if my head would burst when Chris returned my kiss with equal passion, while her young heart raced furiously, exquisitely, against my chest.

Kate's thin, seemingly distant, voice brought us both back to earth with a jolt.

"Knock it off, you two. There's people watching, for heavens sake," she laughingly scolded, "and besides, look at the time; we've got to pack up soon and get off home you wicked pair."

Chris slowly rolled away and lay on her back in the soft sand, breathing heavily, quietly smiling to herself. I sat up and murmured, sheepishly, "Sorry, Kate, we shouldn't have done that, I know, we're a couple of clowns. Awkward for you, isn't it?"

"Don't be so daft." tittered Kate, "I played Cupid, didn't I?" "Where on earth d'you learn that expression, at your age" I sniggered.

"She's not as young as she looks," chuckled Chris, and they both exchanged winks and laughed.

"What would Mamma say?" chortled Kate.

"Why, are y'going to tell 'er?" I cried, with really feigned concern.

"I might, if y'don't behave y'self. Don't try anything when y'think I'm not looking, either," Kate warned. Both girls rolled over on their tummies in the warm sand, laughing loudly at my expense. Playfully, I slapped the backs of Kate's legs. "Oh eh, I'll tell Ma you belted me, as well," Kate chortled. Grinning contentedly, I dropped down on the sand between my two carefree, young companions. All three of us lay there, happily soaking up the sun, before having to pack up and make the long 'trek' home. It really felt good to be alive.

Colwyn Bay sands were always remembered with amusement and very great affection.

CHAPTER 2

Calm before the Storm

As a result of dad's improved job opportunities, some savings and with the help of proceeds from my mum's long invested endowment policy, our foresighted parents managed to buy their first house. The mortgage taken out would cover a period of twenty years but they thought it would be worth the strenuous effort to bring us all a bit of much needed security. At that time, home ownership seemed a good idea if one could only afford it. It might mean a new and better foothold in life for our happy little family; a start on the road to improvement and success. Obviously, a new domestic economic battle lay ahead, but we were all used to struggling for survival and a better future.

So it was that, in the mid-thirties, we moved to our own comfortable, slightly bigger, terrace house on the other side of Penny Lane. A bathroom, with toilet and marvellous electric light throughout the premises, seemed like absolute heaven to Kate and me. I well remember playing with the electric switches - 'on-off, on-off,' until Ma shouted, frantically, "Stop that at once, Bernie, you'll blow us all up, for heaven's sake." Times have changed, haven't they? Having had plenty of practise decorating, we all 'mucked in' and made our new home into a little palace - or so we thought.

At this time, still at school of course, I and several other local lads developed a craze for playing cricket in - of all places - an entry (4ft passage) between the blocks of terrace houses. High gable walls, on either side, prevented damaged windows and as people in nearby property all had kids, I guess they didn't mind the racket. Although Greenbank Park would have been a better spot to play, we lazy little beggars wouldn't walk that far. At times, during our game, young, mischievous girls vexed us by running off with the ball hoping for a chase. One twelve year old rascal, Margaret, was a tiger with a very roving eye for the lads - particularly me. (Hope she wasn't related to Liverpool's famous 'Maggie May'). One day, inducing me to chase her by the usual trick of 'pinching' the ball, she dodged away into our wide entry, out of sight of the other lads and, of course, let me catch her with the ball tightly clutched behind her back against the wall. I grabbed for the ball, as she knew I would, and that started it. Very good looking and well developed for her age, she quickly hugged me close to her and wriggled like a snake, with the expertise and agility of a belly dancer twice her age. I can't say that I didn't enjoy the experience but, at that very moment, my Pa, back from work, cycled down the entry. "What's all this, then? What seems to be goin' on, like?" He shouted and then, as an after-thought to put the girl off, said, "What's our Chris goin' t'say about this?" "Oh, we we're just fooling about, Pa. She - er, sort of pinched the ball from the cricket and well - we, we wanted it back, y'see!" I spluttered, rather lamely.

"Y'don't say," he cried, trying to keep a straight face, "well, that's one 'ruddy' way of putting it, I must say," he concluded, suppressing his mirth. We shot off up the entry, Maggie dropping her hankie as she ran. Picking it up and waving, I shouted after her. Turning, she yelled back, "Bring it round darling, there's a sweetie." and then, quickly, she disappeared into the next street. In my hand was a really fancy, scented, cream coloured handkerchief with the name 'Margaret' in pink stitching and a bold lipstick mark underneath. For several minutes, I stood looking down at the small square piece of silky material and a strong, sweet scent drifted up to my nostrils. Should I return it? I was tempted. Little minx. I knew were she lived. One thing, however, deterred me for I knew that Maggie's mother wore very short skirts, always had strong facial makeup and her appearance really scared me. If she opened the door, I'd die, I truly would.

Although saying to myself that I'd just keep the hankie till I saw Maggie again, the sweet perfume soon changed my mind. Being daft, I resolved to just push the rolled up silk through the letter box and hop it.' What I didn't know was the fact that Maggie's mother was frequently out 'on business' about which the neighbours, apparently, knew a good deal.

Finding the house, I crept, furtively, onto the doorstep and carefully slipped the scented silk under the letter flap! Imagine my sudden shock, when the fancy curtain moved behind the glass panel, the door flew open and young Maggie grabbed my arm. She was completely 'starkers' except for a tiny pair of briefs. With highly comical reaction, I pulled away in sheer panic and raced down the street like a frightened rabbit with a fox in hot pursuit.

Amusingly, after that episode, Maggie still tried to entice me with her charms, but my Pa's rather clumsy attempts at 'facts-of-life' explanations and the oft told hair raising' stories I'd heard, really put a brake on our possible amorous antics.

Smoking (the possible consequences of which we knew nothing) was seen to be manly, a vice common to most of us lads. Up the back entry or anywhere else out of sight, we'd smoke 'woodies' (Woodbines or Weights - at 2d for a packet of five.) When we had the money. Mind you, I turned a bit 'green' after the first on. Wish I'd packed it in then. I did, ten years later. Cigarette cards, the only saving grace of the industry, were a great craze for collectors and very many good sets - about 50 to a set - were produced. 'Black Cat,' 'Craven A' and others issued silk squares depicting flowers, national flags etc. as a variation to cards. I don't regret collecting 'cigy' cards but I'm rather sorry to have pinched birds eggs for my large, glass topped box. (Long since gone, I might add). Although frowned upon today, and rightly so, there is a funny side to this mischievous, one time, boyhood activity.

Soon after nearly falling about twenty feet when trying to reach a crow's nest, I did procure, from a lower level, a couple of sea gulls' eggs which, as everyone knows, are rather large. As everyone also knows, gulls can eat some peculiar things. Well, whether or not this has any bearing on what followed in my story, I'm not quite sure. However, having purloined the eggs, I later proceeded to blow them necessary for preservation - in the back kitchen, at home. (Removing egg contents by blowing through holes made at either end, is a lengthy operation.) Now, my Pa was having a quiet read in the kitchen, while Ma was busy sewing by the fire.

For a moment, as my delicate operation proceeded, everywhere was quiet as the grave and then, all hell broke loose. "What in hell's that!" bellowed Pa, as the ghastly aroma drifted in from the scullery, Pa charged out, closely followed by Ma. "What the devil are y'doing. That stink. You'd think a blasted sewer'd burst." Pa exploded. "You've been at it again, haven't you?" Shouted Ma, eyeing the revolting slime bulging from the gulls egg into an old tin. "Outside! outside! get it out, and don't put it in the bin or we'll never get shut of it." She ordered, sharply. "No, the flaming bin men'll 'ave a fit. They'll go berserk," spluttered Pa.

Sulphuretted hydrogen, if that's what it was certainly caused a great commotion in our house that night and I daren't ever mention egg collecting after that.

Kate's growing interest in nature study caused little criticism as she, thankfully, didn't bring home any noxious specimens, unless one includes young Jack, one of her early boyfriends. My birds' egg collecting phase soon passed as I became interested in photography and the rapidly developing topic of conversation, wireless. Wild life photography commenced with a very simple, second-hand camera, greatly intrigued Kate when I first started the hobby. Capturing birds, their eggs and anything else of natural interest, on film was, to her, a much more acceptable way of keeping and recording the wonders of nature. Kate, herself, took some excellent pictures.

Photographic expertise and electrical knowledge which I quickly gained, proved to be of great value after the War, while an interest in plants became all important during the War. My first job, on leaving school at 15, was in a large garden nursery. In later years, a great deal of much needed produce was raised here when wartime food stocks rapidly began to dwindle. We young apprentice gardeners were allowed time to attend the Liverpool Technical College for study. Along with nursery work, the course included physics and chemistry which appealed to me but not all, I'm afraid. Three young ladies, also attending the classes, were always highly amused by the fact that one teacher, a tall, thin unassuming young man, could be easily embarrassed by a harmless comment in conversation and blush furiously to the roots of his hair. This very pleasant chap and good instructor had, I'm afraid, the unfortunate name of Pratt. Need I say more.

Partial outdoor life seemed to improve my general health, after some initial heart problems and, with study and good hard work, I acquired qualifications which enhanced my job prospects. As a land girl, during the war, Chris joined me in the nursery and, although some incidents occurred which we'd like to forget, we did enjoy amusing and even hilarious events in the oddest places, at all times of the year.

Winter, when we were young, was much more severe than now and I well remember one very hard spell when Kate, Chris and I visited Sefton Park, trudging through crisp, sparkling snow, to see dozens of our fellow Liverpudlians skating on the big lake. Snow-laden branches on trees, covering the more distant hills surrounding the ice covered water, could hardly be seen for a cold, thin, white mist which gripped the whole landscape. “Look at the thickness of that ice,” exclaimed Kate, pointing to a large hole in the frozen lake surface made by park workers for the many ducks skidding around on the smooth, shiny landing patch.’ We couldn’t help laughing at their crazy, unhappy antics.

Six inch thick ice on the lake and twinkling, powdery snow made the park landscape resemble a scene from the Arctic Circle! “Come on!” Shouted Chris, enthusiastically, “let’s get over to the far side in that bay. I’m going to skate.”

“Can you?” I asked, with great surprise.

“Of course,” grinned Chris, obviously relishing my astonishment. Following her across the slippery ice, dodging skaters, we made it, more by luck than judgment, to the far bank and, dusting snow from a seat, sat down shakily. Steel skates soon in position on her strong shoes, Chris was away across the path and on to the ice.

Like a graceful gazelle, she glided smoothly and turned with the expertise of a ballerina, or so it seemed to us, on the bank! “I’d no idea you could skate like that, Chris,” I shouted over, in total admiration; my breath condensing like puffs of smoke in the still, bitterly cold air.

“There’s a lot you don’t know about me, darlin” Chris called back over her shoulder, as she turned and came, with apparent ease, ‘crunch , crunch,’ over the crispy snow, towards our seat.

“She’s good, she really is, she’s great,” I said to Kate. “I know, she’s been practising,” answered Kate, “and she’s going to teach me.”

“How’s that?” enthused Chris, triumphantly, as she reached us and sat down, a little breathless.

“You little secret skater,” I laughed and kissed her full on the lips. “That deserves a kiss, I must say. But why didn’t y’tell me you could skate?”

“I don’t tell you everything, dearie” she joked. “You’d

KATE'S 'ICE S-CREAM SPLIT ON THE FROZEN LAKE-SEFTON PARK. WINTER 1938
TITTER! - TRY AN' KEEP Y'LEGS TOGETHER, KATE!
Y'JOKIN' — DON'T GET FUNNY, BERNIE, I'LL FALL!
OH, DO SHUT UP, BERNIE-DARLIN', YOU'RE A MENACE! — KATE, YOU'RE FINE.
AH, SHE'S ONLY A KID — 'OPE SHE DON'T 'URT HER RUDDY SELF!
OH, GOD! LOOK THE STATE OF 'ER — SHE'LL BE ON HER 'BUM' IN A 'JIFFY'!
SQUAWK
EH, JOE, THAT BIRD'LL BE DOIN' THE 'SPLITS'!
YEAH, SURE WILL — SHOWIN' HER 'DRAWERS'!

know as much as I do. And besides, I needed practise in case I made an utter fool of m'self."

"Oh, you'd never do that," I whispered, softly, stroking her arm.

"Flattery'll get y'nowhere," she laughed, "Come on, Kate, I'll give you a go on the ice, now."

"Oh, d'you think I could? D'you really think I could?" Questioned Kate, rather nervously.

"Of course, I'll fix the skates on and we'll get you over there. Then just take it easy and try to keep your legs together. Looking at both girls with great amusement, I burst out laughing. Trying to keep a straight face, Chris muttered, "You've got a horrible mind, you. Now then, here you are, Kate, we'll just get these on your feet and then I'll help you up."

"What for?" I tittered, "she'll be on her 'bum' again, in a couple of minutes."

"Oh, do be quiet, Bernie, take no notice, Kate, he's just trying to put you off."

"She'll be off alright, OFF along the ice on her drawers," I guffawed, loudly.

"I don't wear drawers," tittered Kate.

"Oh, pardon me," I chuckled, gleefully, "on your bare one, then."

"I didn't mean that either," Kate giggled, and the two girls nearly fell off the seat, quivering with laughter. "I won't be able to do this, if you make us laugh," protested Kate, still giggling.

"You won't be able to do this FULL STOP!" I chortled, once again.

"Give over, will you, Bernie," said Chris, sharply; trying hard not to laugh.

"OK, we'll give it a go," I conceded, mirthfully and stood on one side of Kate, helping her up while Chris took her other arm! Gingerly, all three of us picked our way through the powdery snow to the smooth, uninviting catastrophe zone. Kate, gasping out large vapour clouds, did her very best to stay on her feet and stand up on the skates.

I'll never forget the look on her face when her left leg went 'west' and her right leg 'east,' before she managed to keep her balance for the first time. With one capable helper, Chris, and the other, hopeless me, poor Kate tried desperately to get the hang of it. After several 'bum' slides and a few 'belly flops' she did achieve some success, albeit rather minor and very shaky. And, she was a bit bruised and sore for the next few days. Needless to say, they never saw me with skates on except metaphorically speaking.

Starting out as a trainee hairdresser, Chris, who left school before me, enjoyed the work and progressed very well in the job, before becoming a wartime land-girl.' Prime Minister Chamberlain's 'paper waving' exercise at Heston air-port, at the end of September 1938; after his agreement with Adolf Hitler at Munich, lulled us all into false hopes of 'peace in our time.' Our two families, in keeping with many more, carried on our lives much as usual and just hoped for the best.

Very often Pa and I visited a little barber's shop, (I think mentioned in a Beatles song) at the bottom of Penny Lane hill, for a 'short-back-and-sides,' before Chris took over and cut our hair; partly as a favour to us and also as good practise for her. No, she didn't put a basin on our heads and cut round it, either. Ladies hairdressing was, of course, her main job and she frequently worked on the popular permanent waving styles, 'perms,' for those who could afford them. Invented about 1906, the perm, along with other parts of the business were rapidly evolving and Chris, by her training, soon began to acquire the expertise necessary to become a good hairdresser. Although the War later interrupted her career, she started again, part-time, after hostilities ceased.

Horticulture was, for me and the lads, mostly the growing of flowering plants and fruit, but soon became intensive food production for the War effort. Immediately the War broke out, on September 3rd, 1939, the government launched a great 'grow-more-food' campaign and later a well publicized 'Dig for Victory' drive directed to ordinary folk, particularly 'townies' - townspeople - with the intention of increasing home food production on any bit of spare land available. Before the War, half our food was imported and the amount of land devoted to food production was very low. A very considerable increase was really needed.

All this activity, publicity and great uncertainty was, to us in 1938-39, still very much in the future and we blissfully enjoyed our work and play with all the spirit and enthusiasm born of youth. Chris and I spent a lot of time together, when not working for a small but, nevertheless, welcome wage, and we cycled quite a lot. This was a cheap recreation which we both enjoyed.

A day out across the Mersey - without the bikes - was a change and, one bank holiday, we went to New Brighton on the Royal Iris. It was packed to the gunnels. Bright and sunny, it promised to be a glorious day as we jostled our way to the upper deck with a very large bag of food and a flask. The rumpus aboard the boat is hard to describe. Kids with sweets and lollies dodging one another up and down the decks, while anxious parents - no doubt wishing they could nail their offsprings' boots to the deck - watched and shouted to prevent the young 'tinkers' from taking an unscheduled dip. Middle-aged passengers seemed highly amused at the youngsters antics, until showered with upset lemonade or having their unprotected, sandalled toes stamped on by dozens of undiscerning, scampering little feet.

'I wish I'd brought my box 'Brownie' along," (Kodak camera 12/6 - about 65p) laughed Chris.

"Yes, there's a few good snaps for the album 'ere, I must say," was my reply. "Mind you, Chris, I doubt if you'd stay on y'feet long enough to take'm," Chris nudged me, "Look," she nodded. On the seat opposite, her legs dangling well above the deck, sat a five year old, tousle haired 'Shirley Temple', gobbling licorice allsorts.

"She's got more o'that sweet colour on her face than in her mouth," chuckled Chris, "Her little 'chops' are like a flippin' rainbow."

Shirley Temple's hot, wet, sticky little hand shot up to hide her face as she spotted our amused glances. Peeping shyly at us, between sticky fingers, she suddenly threw back her head and giggled happily, as Chris waved and blew her a kiss. Again galvanized into action, the little girl leaned forward, hands aloft, waving madly, her wild toothy grin revealing a very black licorice coated tongue. In another second, she was off the seat and away down the deck, turning to wave joyously, as she quickly disappeared into the crowd.

"Luvly kid, wish she was mine," sighed Chris.

"You're not old enough, for heaven's sake," I teased.

"Who sez so," returned Chris, with feigned indignation.

"Well, anyway, we can't even afford to get married yet, can we sweetheart?" I questioned.

"Oh, darling, is this a proposal? How romantic, on a boat full of people," Chris chortled.

Sea breeze blew a whisp of Chris's hair across her cheek. Leaning forward, I lifted my hand to smooth the hair back over her temple. As I looked into her clear blue eyes, she didn't move. Soft, warm lips were so inviting and I kissed them, gently. "Will you?" I pleaded, softly. "Will I, what?" she teased. "Oh, when we've got a bit more cash, will you, oh Chris, I luv you will y'marry me, darlin," I blurted out. "There, I've said it. I've always wanted to."

"People are lookin' dear," whispered Chris.

"They can't 'ear, not with all this din goin' on." I answered, squeezing her hand gently. Close to my ear, she said softly, " D'you really want to marry me, Bernie? I mean, it's not just..."

"No, no," I cut in, I'll get more cash in the next couple of years and, and, well, we could live with Ma and Pa for a while I know they wouldn't mind. They think a lot of you, Chris."

" You're serious, aren't y'Bernie? But things might be difficult, y'know. Times are hard."

"Look, Chris, I know life's never easy for us working folk, but time'll pass us by if we don't try luv." These last remarks were so true, my parents obviously realised this when they married.

"I know, Bernie, I do really. We'll have to think it over dear, and decide if we could manage."

"Tell me just one thing, Chris, d'you luv me, really luv me, I mean, enough to marry me?"

People did seem to be watching and an old man, with sideburns, vaguely familiar, smiled across at us and, strangely, appeared to nod his approval. How could he hear us or even, perhaps, read our thoughts. Chris took my hand and whispered, close to my ear, "I luv you, Bernie, I really do. Whatever happens, I do luv you, darling."

"That's all I needed to know. We'll be OK, I know we will," I answered, quietly and, holding her closely, I kissed her again. We didn't care who saw us, we were truly in love.

On the hard wooden seat, we slowly relaxed against the ship's rail and, shyly, I glanced over to the old man with 'side-burns' - he'd gone - but a scrap of paper, trapped by its corner where he'd been sitting, fluttered for just a moment before being swiftly blown past our feet. For some strange reason, I made a grab at it and missed. Instantly the small paper drifted up - up and away over the ship's rail, but, as it did so, I swear that the shakily written capitals 'GOD-SPEED' were just visible on it, as the wind whisked it away and out of sight.

"What's that, that bit of paper. Hope it wasn't a bank note," exclaimed Chris.

"Oh, nothing, I guess, just a scrap of lunch paper, the old man left behind. He smiled at us, remember; perhaps he left us his good wishes on it." I laughed, rather awkwardly. Looking at me very curiously, Chris stammered, "What old man, what good wishes. I've only seen 'our Shirley Temple' with her sweet bag. You've got a vivid imagination, you have, me-lad. It's all this sea air and marriage proposal lark's gone to y'head." Chris grabbed me tightly and kissed me hard on the cheek, as two little kids stopped to watch! "I do luv you," she chuckled, "imagination and all, you funny old thing." The two children ran off giggling, looking back and pointing. "Them's luvvers." One young lad shouted, loudly. Chris also heard him and laughed, "Well, he might be right, at that, mightn't he?" "What do you think, my darling?" I answered.

Soon, New Brighton loomed ahead and Chris, still with picnic bag, clung to my arm as we made our way towards the gangway. With the ferry boat securely tied and bobbing gently against the landing stage, the gang plank thudded down and, with hordes of laughing, noisy holiday makers, we pushed and jostled our way ashore. Reaching the pier, thronged with happy visitors of every conceivable shape and size, Chris and I suddenly looked at one another and burst out laughing, when two rather oversize ladies complete with very large kids balloons gleefully sauntered by. "The things y'see, when y'haven't got a gun," I exploded.

"Look, there's plenty more where they came from." Chris giggled, pointing to the motley crowds surrounding the photo booths, fortune tellers tents and penny slot machines. It really was a glorious, typical holiday scene of the times, and absolutely everybody was rollickingly happy.

Bernie Pykett, the well-known one legged diver, who regularly leapt from New Brighton Pier into the icy waters of the Mersey, was a great attraction and very amusing to us. Whether the cold bath was as funny to him, I'm not so sure.

Perhaps his favourite catch phrase, "Every penny makes the water warmer." Really did work. He certainly deserved every penny he got and he got quite a few, believe me. Incidentally, Tommy Handley's I.T.M.A. radio show, in 1939, remembered the diver when, well known Jack Train used to call out gruffly, "Don't forget the diver, sir - don't forget the diver." Happy days! Chris often ribbed me about jumping off the pier - my name being Bernie. Little devil, I think she knew that I couldn't swim.

Although the New Brighton Tower was dismantled in 1919 (considered to be a landmark for the German Zeppelins during World War I) the Tower grounds remained for a number of years with a ballroom and fairground type amusements still available. Leaving the pier, we made our way through the teeming crowds to the Tower entertainments for a brief visit. Unbelievably jostled by boisterous humanity, we soon laughingly decided to seek slightly quieter, calmer, 'pastures new.'

Past the old fort, (once guarding the estuary of the Mersey) we strolled down the prom heading towards the Red Noses (a sandstone bulge projecting from the coastal hillside). Everywhere, along the prom, on the sand and rocks, in front of the fort and lighthouse, people milled around in their hundreds enjoying the glorious sunshine and invigorating sea air, whilst making the most of every minute of their one day holiday at the seaside. One day, free from the cares and worries of daily life, was all that many, here today, would enjoy for many months to come. Holidays, real holidays were something that few people could afford or even contemplate. Bank Holiday was really the only break from the daily 'grind,' a great fun day out for the 'world and his wife.'

Finding a quiet spot for our picnic lunch was very nigh impossible, so we settled for a sunny patch of grass, near the prom, where not too many folks had the same idea. Nothing much ever happened to spoil our simple outings and we always enjoyed ourselves. Although lots and lots of people were usually around, one never felt uneasy or threatened. Most people just wanted a good day out, a happy time without causing bother to anyone else.

Linking arms with Chris, as we journeyed home, I felt on top of the world. Chris's love, so tenderly declared, meant a great deal to me. This had been my special day and, with all my heart, I wanted to marry Chris. Until now, I hadn't fully realised how close we'd become, how much I really needed her. Apart from her attractive physical appearance. Chris's wonderful personality, inner warmth, straightforward honesty and practicality, were qualities much admired and, I felt, could greatly enhance our married happiness; our future life together. Chris was a lovely person, a girl of whom one could be justly proud.

Circumstances making it difficult for us to achieve our dream of a normal, happy married life together, we took every opportunity, time permitting, to enjoy ourselves without spending too much money. (Undoubtedly, one needed reasonable savings for a decent future). Kate, although sometimes with us, was now studying hard and hoped very much to become a nurse. Her being away for training, in the not too distant future, saddened me a little as we were so close and she'd never been away from home before. I knew we'd all miss her dreadfully when the time came, but her mind was made up and I felt, in my heart, that she was right to choose nursing as a career.

A journey with Chris on Liverpool's great little Overhead Railway reminded me of the same trip enjoyed by Kate and me when we were still at school. Stretching from Dingle to Seaforth, this novel and exciting electric railway gave one a fine, elevated view of River Mersey's multifarious activities and the many strange and interesting scenes on both banks of a very busy river.

Strongly built in 1893, this great coastal railway, built twenty feet above ground level and serving twenty one stations

Liverpool Overhead Railway, the 'Docker's Umbrella'-1893-1956.
For Docks & Liners
Liverpool-Overhead-Railway
Sport-Seaforth-Dingle
Finest Scotch Whisky
Liverpool-Ove
Railway
Liverpool Overhead Railway
Seaforth
23
Train crossing St. Nicholas' Place
Bow-string girder bridge, Liverpool
Young
Bernie and Kate waiting to board
the 'Overhead'
at Seaforth-Litherland
station - 1938.

along its length, was dismantled after the Second World War; which seems a great pity, it would have been a good tourist attraction now. Demolition proved to be quite a task, due to very solid construction, which is probably a tribute to the old builders.

Prior to the War, boat trips to North Wales were frequently advertised and so Chris and I, having 'wangled' a free day together from work, decided to grab the opportunity and go for a sail. Leaving Liverpool landing stage on a gloriously calm summer's day, the St. Seriol II with us aboard, set sail, bound for Llandudno and the pleasant Isle of Anglesey.

Compared to a ferry boat, the St Seriol was quite a large vessel and we loved the extra spacious deck space. Strolling hand-in-hand, we made our way to the, seemingly, high ship's bows to enjoy the really delightful, bracing sea air of Liverpool Bay, as the boat cruised smoothly onwards towards its first port of call, Llandudno. With shrieking gulls circling above and invigorating, warm wind sweeping past our faces, it just felt marvellous to be aboard.

"Oh, God, isn't it great, this air," Chris shouted loudly, against the wind. "I'd luv, to be a sailor," she laughed.

"Today's fabulous," I bellowed back, "but what about when the gales are blowin,' you wouldn't want to be a sailor then, y'little townie."

"Spoil sport," she hollered, turning round as the wind blew brown locks of hair across her pretty face. Seizing her in my arms, as she leaned against the rail, I gently pushed a wisp of hair aside and kissed her full on the lips. In a high, falsetto voice, I chirped, "I luv you, sailor." With an equally artificial laugh, she giggled, "I bet you say that to all the sailors."

"Only the really good lookin' ones," I chuckled.

"Flatterer," she sniggered, "Come on, darlin', let's go and sit down," she whispered, close to my ear. "We'll 'ave plenty of walkin' when we arrive, won't we?"

We had food with us for a snack, but I knew a little cafe, in Llandudno, which served very nice meals at a reasonable price. On this occasion, by deciding to stay in the town until the boat returned from Anglesey, we'd have much more time to browse around this great little seaside resort. In brilliant sunshine we landed during early afternoon and really enjoyed our bracing walk from the boat stage along the lengthy Pier. To the right, looming above us, in all its splendour, the Great Orme's Head dominated the landscape, while to our left, over the pier rail, we could see the lovely and impressive bay sweeping away towards the Little Orme, a couple of miles along the coast. Dotted along the pier, small kiosks sold sweetmeats, rock, drinks and cakes, while souvenirs, such as named ornaments, shells and countless other items - to delight visitors gaze - were on display, for sale. Of course, I had to purchase a pretty little ornament which caught Chris's eye as a memento of our happy visit. (We still have it now, I believe.)

Reaching the very large, impressive promenade (must be one of the best in North Wales), we trotted along to Mostyn Street, the main shopping area, and found our small, cosy cafe in a side street.

"It's really nice 'ere, I must say," Chris whispered, during a very enjoyable meal, "how d'you find it?"

"Oh, we all came 'ere a couple of years ago," I replied, "and, as y'can see, the prices aren't bad at all, are they?"

"No, great!" grinned Chris, "We'll jolly well have to come 'ere again, some day, Bernie."

A wee bit pushed for time, we left the cafe and slowly ambled up, past the imposing Grand Hotel, towards a raised promenade leading to the very pleasant Happy Valley Gardens. Mingling with the many sunburnt holiday makers, we thrilled to the magnificent views across the bay from this lovely sunny slope! Bathing in warm sunshine, whilst admiring enchanting scenery from a seat on our 'lofty perch,' the time just seemed to fly like a bird on the wing.

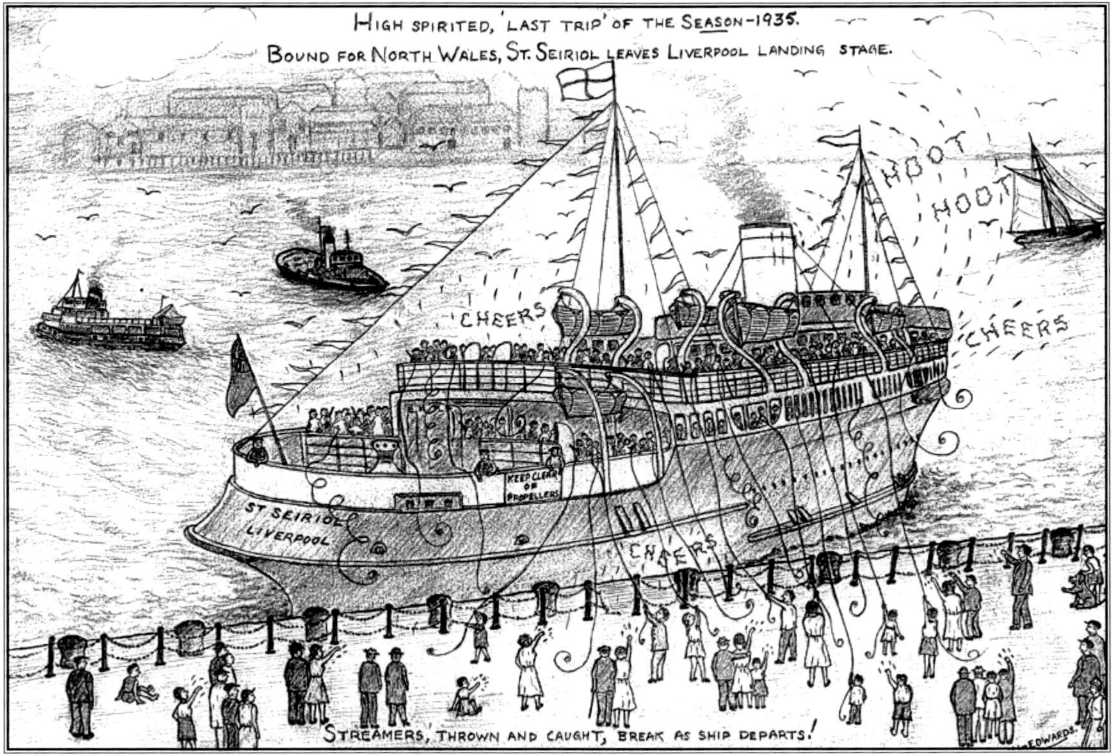
HIGH SPIRITED, 'LAST TRIP' OF THE SEASON-1935.
BOUND FOR NORTH WALES, ST. SEIRIOL LEAVES LIVERPOOL LANDING STAGE.
HOOT
HOOT
CHEERS
CHEERS
CHEERS
KEEP CLEAR OF PROPELLERS
ST SEIRIOL
LIVERPOOL
STREAMERS, THROWN AND CAUGHT, BREAK AS SHIP DEPARTS!
EDWARDS

I'd luv to stay 'ere, Bernie," Chris murmured, lazily looking out to sea, "but shouldn't we see a bit of the prom, before goin' back? We 'aven't got a lot of time left, 'ave we?"

"You're dead right, I'm afraid, luv. The boat's due back in less than an hour, so we'd better get down, I s'pose." Back at road level, we sauntered along the wide, hotel lined, promenade thronged with jovial visitors all in holiday mood and, despite packed seats near colourful, prom flower borders, we did find a space to sit and enjoy a few laughable moments watching comical antics of delighted kids and their amused parents, cavorting down on the crowded beach, making the most of their short holiday.

They, like us, were so very blissfully unaware of the ominously, gathering clouds of war about to engulf everyone in these islands. For this, you see, was the summer of 1939.

"D'you know, Bernie, I'd luv to live 'ere, wouldn't you?" Chris beamed, enthusiastically. Listening to the leisurely waves gently caressing the shore and thoughtfully watching gulls swooping down over the pier, I replied, perhaps with premonition "Maybe we will someday, but it might be a very long time, Chris luv!" Chris took my arm and affectionately squeezed my hand.

"Oh, Bernie, it would be luvly, though, wouldn't it?" she whispered, softly.

"Yeah, well, the dream could come true," I answered, little realising the trauma of future years.

All too soon, our lovely afternoon was nearly over and so, reluctantly and with faltering footsteps, we wandered off to catch the boat back home. Though sad at leaving, we had enjoyed another 'super' day, happy recollections, soon to be locked away in our memories, which, whatever happened in the future, nothing could ever erase, not even the frightening events about to unfold before the year's end.

Unlike our day in Wales, ending happily, 1939 drew very

slowly to a peculiarly, unreal conclusion hard for us to comprehend, even to believe. Rumours of war and frightening newspaper headlines made us all very wireless conscious. Constantly listening to newscasts, we hoped and prayed to hear news and some sign that would indicate an improvement in the already rapidly deteriorating situation, something, anything that would avert, what seemed to be an utter disaster. A catastrophe of the first magnitude.

Not surprisingly, on that well remembered Sunday morning, September 3rd 1939, we all huddled round the old home-made wireless set to listen for a special message at 11.15 am from the Prime Minister, Neville Chamberlain which was broadcast to the Nation. Everyone listened, with bated breath, as Mr Chamberlain made his historic broadcast. Although the message, delivered from Downing Street, lasted for several minutes and contained references to his efforts to save peace and the prospects we all would have to face, the few words at the beginning and those at the end of Mr. Chamberlain's last paragraph were the ones which really sank so deeply into our minds. Unless by 11 o'clock that morning, an assurance was given that German troops would be withdrawn from Poland, a state of war would exist between us, (Britain and Germany).

I can still hear Mr. Chamberlain's solemn voice as he said quietly and very gravely, "I have to tell you now that no such undertaking has been received and that consequently this country is at war with Germany!"

For several moments, in a numbed silence, we just sat looking at each other. Kate, always abhorring violence and cruelty, was deathly pale. What would it all mean what would happen, what would Hitler and the Germans do? And when? What would we do. Was our small country really ready for a ghastly, terrifying war. These fleeting, frightening thoughts must have passed through all our minds, as the old wireless droned on and on, without a listener. We were all just utterly devastated.

Life had never been a bed of roses for anyone but, at least, it was reasonably quiet and normal. Now, it seemed, that our passable, humdrum little world was beginning to collapse around our ears. Everyone's lives, including ours, could be completely shattered, without a doubt.

Sudden silence when Pa, white faced, switched off the wireless, triggered an immediate and very confused conversation, as we all gabbled at once seeking to explain, to find answers, to make sense of this frightening and catastrophic situation. The very chaotic nature of our talk was akin to the utter chaos into which, it now seemed, the whole Nation was about to be plunged.

Living through the First World conflict, our parents had witnessed the horrors of war. Pa had been wounded and Ma was nearly killed by a sabotage bomb in a munitions factory. They both had seen the shattered bodies and shell shocked casualties returned from Verdun, Ypres, the Somme and many other places. Ma, we knew, in keeping with countless other mothers, had hoped for better times for their kids; for all of us. And now this. Tears, dimming her kind grey eyes, reflected the deep hurt, the sadness and fear that she felt. She must have realised, too, that this approaching war was destined to be far worse, in many ways, than World War I.

The, now rather laughable, Zeppelins reached and bombed London, but most of the unbelievable carnage took place in France, Belgium and Germany - far away from home - during the First War. In 1940 a frighteningly different situation would face us all. No-one anywhere would be safe! Hitler's well trained millions, his large air force, possible unknown weapons and his insane desire for European domination, presented a frightening prospect and very fearful thoughts for everyone in these Precious Islands! Although none of us voiced the opinion, I'm sure we all realised that Britain, at this time, was unprepared and had very little with which to fight.

Never will I forget the grave expressions, the feelings of

helpless resignation in all our hearts and minds, just after the sickening declaration of war, while listening to that first broadcast to the Nation made by a sad, bitter, disillusioned and very disappointed man - Mr. Neville Chamberlain. Unknown to us then, we faced five long years of total War. By a miracle, Britain, badly mauled, managed to survive. I hope, she always will. These are Great Little Islands.

CHAPTER 3

One Bright Event Lightens Dark Days

Radio waves carried many depressing messages over the next five years, but wireless wasn't always disheartening and it provided us with a great deal of very pleasurable entertainment during those, otherwise, dispiriting dark days and nights of war. Quite literally, nights really were very dark, for blackout regulations came into force immediately war had been declared. On September 4th, after Ma and Kate had found suitable material, Pa and I began the task of fitting black-out curtains to all the windows and sticking special linen tape (bought earlier by Pa as a precaution to any unprotected glass) in the rather vain hope of 'splinter' protection, in case of a bomb blast.

Expecting air raids at any time - London had a false warning half an hour after War was declared - we lived a sort of double life; normal on the one hand and yet with a strange sense of nervous uncertainty on the other. Ever present in our minds was the horror of merciless bombing and air-borne invasion. In fact, no real raids took place until six weeks later, on Monday 16th of October - when German planes tried to bomb ships in the Firth-of-Forth. Scapa Flow was attacked the following day. Liverpool, however, and many other places didn't suffer initial air raids and, apart from our involvement in preparations and precautions - fire watching, air raid precautions (A.R.P.), Wardens service and the like, life seemed , more or less, normal. Drifting along, we learned to live with the suspense and soon dubbed these early months, the 'phoney war'. Large temporary 'dug-out' air raid shelters - covered with planks and earth - were constructed in many parks whilst we, at the garden nursery, started on the big change over to intensive food production.

In her final year at school, Kate wasn't evacuated and hoped to earn a good report so that she might be accepted for tuition at a nurses' training school. Some nurses are made; Kate, to me, was a born nurse. Caring and compassionate, she liked people and was quick to learn. She had great determination and - so important for a nurse - she wasn't easily daunted. She's my kid sister and I'm very proud of her.

Many, many school children and people considered to be vulnerable, were evacuated to places of safety. Crowds of kids lined up for trains, buses, coaches and even steamers for their journey into the unknown. Some youngsters were excited, some uncertain and tearful, but all were, noticeably, carrying a small square cardboard gas mask box, slung from their shoulders by a string. Everyone was issued with these simple gas masks except the Home Guard, Wardens and similar services, who were given larger, more cumbersome types. Looking back, I think that the value of the simple masks was more psychological than real! If a serious gas attack had taken place - phosgene, mustard or any other ghastly chemical that Hitler might have had, and used then, I think, we'd all have been in deep trouble. Like many serious things, there was a funny side to gas masks. When worn, they looked strange and a nose outlet valve made a queer noise when one breathed.

When I first tried on the mask, Chris, with her wry sense of humour, said laughingly, as she beat a hasty retreat, "You certainly look better with it on, darling." Fair comment on quite a few individuals I chanced to meet on my travels.

Food rationing soon became part of daily life and Ma had charge of the small card backed ration books, filled with 'fiddley' little coupons to be cut out and used to obtain all the basic foods. One did, I hasten to add, need money as well as the coupons! As we were never very 'well off,' I don't suppose rationing made a great deal of difference except that we did get our fair share.

Chris, her family and ours, sometimes used to listen in on

the wireless to that Irish 'twit,' William Joyce - employed by the Germans to peddle spurious propaganda to Britain. Lord Haw-Haw, as he came to be known, due to his patronizing tone of voice, was a constant topic of conversation. I don't think that his attempts at half-truth subversion ever worked. He was a bit of a laugh really, and the British troops caught up with him in Hamburg at the end of the War, and the 'little weasel' was later hanged for treason (I hope he went to the right place; Hell's concert party, perhaps).

As a result of the government's appeal for more food production, the Women's Land Army came into being and that's how Chris got involved and became a land girl. Being already in the job, I managed to persuade my nursery to take her on as a trainee. With some knowledge of gardening, my help and the training Chris received in the nursery, she soon became a very efficient worker. Working for the same firm seemed an ideal situation for both of us. Obviously, we didn't always find jobs together - it was a big place - but meal breaks often helped us to keep in touch, depending on where our jobs happened to be.

Everything, one might say, in the garden was looking 'rosy' but, as always, there was a slight snag. That 'snag' took the form of the boss's nephew, Ben. Right from the start, I noticed that Ben kept eyeing Chris with more than just a friendly glance! He obviously fancied her; he really did. Initially, Chris and I joked about it, but awkward moments did sometimes occur. Although Chris didn't invite his attentions, she had to be reasonably civil to him; after all he was the boss's 'blue eyed boy'. Ben, not bad in many ways, knew that I was going out with Chris but didn't seem - didn't want - to take it seriously. I imagine he thought that being the owner's nephew might give him 'the edge.' From my long friendship with Chris, I knew that any words or advances made by Ben - or anyone else - would fall on deaf ears. He didn't know my Chris. Nevertheless, this possible threat to our happiness - plus an unexpected turn of events in the War - did bring our engagement that much closer.

It was early June, 1940, and the evacuation of Dunkirk had just been completed - with terrible loss of life. Thoughts in all our minds were of this disastrous setback and its possible consequences. Last September's gloom descended once again and we prayed for a change in Britain's fortunes. Long, fairly sunny days helped to raise our spirits as Chris and I continued to work at the nursery. One day, with a little connivance on my part, we were both picking and collecting tomatoes in the same large glass house. Not a bad job but for the fact that hands, work coats and even hair got covered with a yellow-green dye, whilst moving up and down between the 'tommy' plants.

Just out of sight, lower down the greenhouse, I could hear our workmate, June, moving about while Chris, her nimble fingers busy on the ripening fruit, was weaving her way amongst dozens of tomato plants on a nearby raised, central bed. Walking up the well worn brick path, my head almost level with her waist, I approached Chris as she stopped work to look down at me.

"How's it goin' Chris. Had enough?"

"Y'can say that again," Chris grinned, "Just look at these hands - they're green as grass!"

"Ah, poor soul," I sniggered, with mild sarcasm.

"I'm wearing some sort of gloves on this job, next time" complained Chris. Standing near the edge of the raised bed, she slipped off a shoulder strap and lowered the tomato basket to the soil. "Phew! That's better; they're gettin' awful heavy," she murmured.

Being well above the path, her lovely legs were so very close to me. Suddenly, I grabbed her round the waist and nestled my head against her middle.

"Hey! Knock it off, for goodn' sake," Chris exclaimed, in great surprise, "Suppose the foreman comes in. Our John'll have a fit if he sees you up to y'tricks, mi lad." she cried.

"I don't care, Chris," I said, looking up at her, "Let's, let's get engaged."

"What! You do have the happy knack of being romantic in the strangest places," giggled Chris. "No, I'm serious, Chris," I lowered my head and gently kissed her tummy. My hands drifted down behind her legs to stroke those shapely calves.

"Oh, God! Chris, y'know how it is, with the War and everything; we don't know what'll happen, do we?" I whispered, despairingly, looking up again into her, now, tear filled eyes.

"You're a good man, Bernie, and y'know I luv you, darling - and, yes - yes, if it'll make you happy; we'll get engaged. I know the time's goin' so quick."

"Will it make you happy, Chris? Will it, really, Chris, darling" I asked urgently.

"You know it will, y'know very well, it will." she replied, softly and bent down to kiss my cheek. A sudden noise made us move apart and look towards the far end of the greenhouse. No one was there; an unlatched door had just drifted open and hit the brickwork.

"Look, Chris," I said quickly, fumbling in my overall pocket. "I've got you this, I hope y'like it." Fetching out a tiny black box, I held it close to her as she stepped down onto the path. Peering, for a second, at the small square box, she smiled and her eyes filled again as she guessed what it was. Slowly, I opened the lid to reveal a thin gold ring on which was mounted a small diamond, surrounded by tiny rubies!

"Oh, Bernie, it, it's really luvly." Happy tears trickled down Chris's cheeks. "But y'can't afford that now, Bernie, can you?"

"Oh, yes, I can, I saved up, didn't I?" I exclaimed, with pride.

"How on earth did y'know the size t'get?" Chris chuckled, recovering from her initial surprise.

"Ah! now, well, I pinched that dress ring you wear and a chap in the shop gave me one the same size. It's alright though kid, I did put the dress ring back."

"You sneaky beggar," Chris laughed, "What can I say? Except, I LOVE YOU, darling." Chris drew me closely to her and, in a loving embrace, we sealed our bond with a passionate kiss.

Still clutched in my hand, behind Chris's back, the ring,

in its open box, sparkled there for all to see. Oblivious to the fact that June had quietly appeared on the scene, we suddenly heard a very small voice say, "That's really nice, is that for me?"

Quickly breaking away and catching sight of June, we all started laughing.

"You've been 'earwiggin' again, Chris chortled.

"No, honest. Well, yes," June blushed, "I did 'ear somebody say, I love you," she giggled. "Now I couldn't miss that opportunity to 'peek,' could I?

"I s'pose not." tittered Chris, grabbing the little box from me and thrusting it under June's nose. "Well, what d'you think? Isn't it great?"

"I think it's absolutely marvellous, Chris, I do really, but aren't y'goin' to let him put it on y'finger?" asked June.

"Yes, well, I can't now, can I, look at mi fingers; all green with these 'bloomin' tomatoes." Chris replied, trying to wipe stained hands on her apron.

"That doesn't matter, does it?" I laughed. "It's 'aphrodisiac,' juice of the 'Luv Apple'."

"What are you on about?" laughed Chris, "He'll tell you anything; this fella, honestly." she said, nudging June.

"Not at all! Didn't you know the tomato was a luv- apple? It induces amorous desires in the unsuspecting female." I sniggered, with a very broad grin.

"Oh, does it, now, you don't 'flippin' say." They both nearly collapsed laughing.

"Eh, up! John's just cum in the bottom door." June exclaimed, in a loud whisper, as she quickly disappeared over to the middle 'tommy' bed. I took Chris's basket and mine over to the garden trolley and brought back an empty one for her.

"Everything OK?" John called out, a look of impatience on his tanned, rugged face.

"Yes, we've got a good load, we're gettin' through them" I shouted back, cheerily.

"Yes, well, try and speed it up a bit, will you, we're a bit pushed for time, y'know, Bernie."

"OK, will do," I answered, trying to sound efficient, while slyly winking at Chris. As John vanished through the top door, Chris murmured, quietly, "You'll get us all the sack, you with your amorous antics."

"It was you and June laughin' he 'eard. You'll both 'ave to be gagged," I grinned.

"Oh, will we, sez you. We'll see about that" she answered with a very quiet laugh. I blew her a big kiss and we both tried to hurry the job along to keep John and the customers happy.

At the far end of the potting sheds, an 'earthy smelling' cook-house or 'bothy' as we called it with wooden forms, a long table and an old iron kitchen range with oven, and a very well worn stone floor, served as a meal room for the employees. It was used mostly in the wintertime during bad weather, if one needed a hot meal or, as now, when Chris and I happened to be in a nearby glasshouse. Excitedly, we both wanted to sit at the table, talk and see that twinkling, shiny band of gold on her finger. Walking through the potting shed, we were surprised - being lunch-time - to see Tom turning a compost mix on the bench and foreman, John and young June already seated at the 'bothy' table, smirking. Fred, walking in behind us, went over to the decrepit old sink to wash his hands.

All our workmates, including John, found it hard to keep straight faces as we sat down. It was fairly obvious June had 'blown the whistle.' Chris, blushing furiously and nervously looking at her hands, said, "Better wash mine, when you've finished, Fred; my hands an' arms are green as grass after those 'tomies.'" June, grinning broadly, looked at me and John, uttering a strange artificial cough, winked at Tom. "I can see somebody green with envy." Fred murmured quietly, drying his hands, and then quickly added, loudly, "There now, Chris, the sink's all yours, and get that left hand clean, gel, it could be important!" June's infectious laugh set us all off.

"Alright! - Alright," Chris giggled, "I know she's told you. 'Blabber-mouth!" she laughed, playfully hitting young June.

"Well, come on, hurry up," urged John," and get those tiny hands washed; the suspense is killing me."

Chris obliged as they all teased her about wedding bells and 'the Big Day' to come. Fishing the little box out of my overall pocket, I put it on the table and, as Chris sat down, opened it up for all to see. "Isn't it really luvly, I told you t'was a good'n!" cried June, excitedly.

"Oh, God! yes, you've really done her proud, son." John exclaimed, "It's very, very nice, I must say." And I feel sure he meant what he said.

Tom picked up the box and he and Fred eyed its sparkling qualities, under the light, with obvious admiration. "It's one of the best I've seen," said Tom and Fred agreed, enthusiastically.

Chris, I could see, was 'itching' to try on the small token which meant so much to her. June, too, was all agog. "Oh, gosh, do try it Chris. I can't wait to see it on y'finger," she said, impatiently. "Yes, do the decent thing, old son," Tom chuckled as he handed me the box, "and make that beautiful young lady really happy"

Chris held out her hand, while blushing to the roots of her hair. Nervously, I withdrew the ring from its cushion and, as Fred murmured, "With this ring, I thee wed." I pushed the glistening band of love onto Chris's outstretched finger. For a very brief moment, there was complete silence as Chris proudly displayed the diamond, ruby studded ring; beautiful as the lovely girl, herself. 'Congratulations' suddenly the cry was on everyone's lips and John laughingly urged, "Come on now, son, kiss your lovely young bride to be."

"Yes, seal it with a kiss, you two," June echoed. Slightly embarrassed, I drew Chris to me and kissed her lips.

"Oh, you can do better than that." Fred chided, "One more time, and show the 'gel' you really mean it."

Holding Chris closely, I warmly kissed her again as she closed her eyes and, for an instant, we seemed to be really alone. "Luv you, Chris," I whispered. "Luv you, Bernie," she murmured.

"That's better," praised Fred, "And we all hope you'll enjoy a great life together when you do really 'tie the knot.–"

"Yes, course we do," June quickly hugged and kissed Chris and then turned to kiss me, too.

"Look, we haven't got any champagne, right now," cried John,"but a little cafe in High Street might and I'd like you all to join me there for a meal, to mark Chris and Bernie's engagement."

"Gee. Thanks John, "Chris exclaimed, her tear filled eyes sparkling with happy appreciation.

"But we haven't told our folks yet."

"No problem, "John replied, "Just have a word and we'll work out some arrangements." Maybe we'd all rather misjudged poor John, he didn't seem such a 'bad old stick after all. Hardly had our little confab started, when in walked - of all people - Ben, followed by land girl. Heather. "Thought I'd find you here, John," Ben said, "Just wanted a word about that next load, this afternoon."

"Yes, well, before we settle that, I've got a bit of good news, you might like to hear," John cut in, a really impish smile crossing his strong, mature face. "Young Bernie, here and Chris have just become engaged." His grin broadened, as he added, "Don't you think they make a grand young couple?"

Heather leapt forward, kissing Chris and me and voicing her very warm congratulations to us both. To say that Ben's face was a 'study,' is a complete understatement. His jaw dropped, he blushed furiously and it was several seconds before he managed to pull himself together and say, " Oh, I, yes, I do, really," he stammered, while proffering a rather reluctant hand to us, in felicitation. After the 'flabby' hand-shake, he seemed a little more composed and kissed Chris on the cheek, saying, awkwardly, "I, er, hope you'll be happy, Chris." Turning to me, almost as an afterthought, he said, rather coldly, "And you, too, Bernie." There were quite a few amused smiles all round.

With due fairness to Ben, he did, from then on, keep his distance, so to speak, from Chris and didn't make any 'naughty' advances. Something that might not have happened in the 'swinging' sixties.'

Everyone at home, of course, approved of my buying the ring - although they hadn't seen it and knew about the surprise for Chris. Being pals for so long, it had been obvious that we'd soon become engaged. Our two families always expected us to marry some day. Wedding bells, however, we all knew, might be a little way 'down the road' due to the usual money problems and the really very uncertain War outlook. A small family 'get together,' to celebrate our betrothal, was made possible by pooling wartime rations and we, together with a couple of friends and our two families, all managed to enjoy a very pleasant evening party. That little gold band, studded with very small precious stones, which Chris now wore, undoubtedly brought us so much closer; we were virtually married - or so it seemed to us. Over sentimental? perhaps, but I wish that other young couples, today, could share some of that sentiment of ours; some of that tender emotion we both enjoyed at a crucial period in our lives. Money was very short, it was wartime with little more than the basic foods available, but we really loved each other and that's all that seemed to matter.

During our engagement week, we were twice lucky because John, the foreman, proved good as his word and provided the appetizing meal he promised for all of us and our close workmates, which gave Chris and me a great deal of pleasure. In an attractive restaurant, friendly chat and the company of folks who really wished us well, was a glorious change for us during times when a meal out was an absolute luxury. Never did we ever forget John's more than generous gesture and the very memorable engagement party he arranged. Thanks to John 'footing' the party bill, more hard earned savings would be available for the approaching wedding and our 'setting up home' together.

Not so long after our engagement, poor old Pa took ill with a very painful and, to us, frightening complaint, 'quinsy' which affects the throat and tonsils. Young people, in whom it usually occurs, can suffer quite badly but Pa, being middle-aged, really had a rough time. His present sad plight reminded me of my own early childhood battle with the dreaded diphtheria. Never ill and always active, Pa had no option now but to take to his bed, completely prostrated, in severe pain and with a temperature of nearly 103. Hardly able to swallow - I knew the feeling - and with swollen glands, Pa was 'going through the mill.'

It was at this time, I began to realise that Kate had chosen her right vocation. Instinctively, she seemed to know how best to help Pa and cared for him until he was better. One amusing incident occurred when a nursing friend brought a tin of *Antiphlogistine* for poulticing. (Known simply as '*Antiphlo*') Ma puffed up my Pa's pillow and mentioned that the nurse was bringing *Antiphlo* to ease the pain. Being so ill, hardly able to speak and not knowing what on earth she was on about, he tried to say, "Who the hell's Auntie Flo?" Kate and Ma, although worried, nearly-collapsed laughing and tried to explain to him that *Antiphlo* was a poultice for the bad throat. It seemed to work and caused the abscess to burst, giving dear old Pa immediate relief.

For months to come, nurse Joan, who'd first introduced Pa to Antiphlogistine, was laughingly referred to, by Pa, as 'Auntie Flo.' After a short period of convalescence, he made a good recovery but he never forgot '*Antiphlo*,' the nurse who helped to cure his quinsy.

Apart from the humour of Tommy Handley's I.T.M.A programme - started 12th July 1939 - on the wireless and shows like *Hi-gang*, with Bebe Daniels, Ben Lyon and Vic Oliver, which started on May 26th, 1940; laughs and jokes were in very short supply. The shadow of Dunkirk, France's capitulation and armistice with Germany, signed on the 22nd June, gave us very little to smile about. And, soon after Pa's illness, the horror of German air-raids, on North of England towns, very quickly became apparent. On 15th December, the Sheffield area and other parts were heavily attacked in very frightening night raids. By the 20th of December, it was our turn again and, on that night, raiders were over most parts of Britain. We, in Liverpool, had already suffered the heaviest raid of the War on the 28th of November and more since then, but these mid-December raids were extremely bad, with a great deal of damage and, sadly, many, many casualties.

Heart rending scenes, we never thought to see, with high explosive and incendiary bombs raining down from the night skies, were events we all had prayed would never happen. High explosive bombs and land-mines were utterly devastating in effect - as can be imagined - but the subsequent showers of incendiaries later dropped that frightful night, were to us, the survivors left to cope, a terrifying prospect. Fierce fire, molten magnesium and - even worse - an odd explosive 'booby' bomb in every 'stick' (cluster). Miraculously, during two nights of heavy attack, our area received only two or three large bombs, but was straddled by incendiaries. Every local service -Wardens, A.R..P, Police and Fire Service was strained and stretched to the limit in frantic efforts to rescue injured, save life and prevent or extinguish fires; perhaps only able to contain them.

Out with the rest that night, Pa and I escaped serious injury by a 'hairs-breadth,' not just from fire, but by Mr 'Schickelgruber's,' Hitler's cunning device, the explosive incendiary bomb.

Five fire bombs dropped in our street; two went through roofs and were dealt with, one fell in the road while the fourth landed on a cill smashing the window and igniting the frame; the last one hit a front door and set it ablaze. With sandbags and loaded buckets, Pa and I quickly attempted to quench the molten mass of fire. Sand from my first bucket hit the door and slid right on to the bomb. In a split second, as Pa raised a sandbag ready for the throw, I knew, instinctively, that the thing was going to blast. "Run - God, it's going to blow," I yelled. Next thing, we were both laying in the road! Stunned, scratched, bleeding and showered with burning debris, we lay for several minutes before neighbours ran over and took us to a nearby house. Apart from losing some hair, his eyebrows and receiving a few cuts and scratches, Pa wasn't badly injured. Cut and slightly burnt from falling fire remnants, I was shocked and somewhat unsteady because of an earlier knee injury made painful by my sudden, heavy fall on the road. After Kate's quick first-aid, we both resumed our air-raid patrol.

Despite continuing raids, after our bomb scare, no further 'heavies' fell close by and, as the drone of German aircraft receded with the gradually lightening night sky, the glorious sound of an 'All-Clear' filled the air and slowly lifted our flagging spirits. The immense relief, as soft, peaceful light of a new dawn approached, and the indescribable feeling of utter thankfulness just to be alive - can only be fully appreciated by someone who has lived through the trauma of such ghastly nights. Realising we'd all survived another night's dreadful ordeal, our minds tended to conjure up scenes of carnage which, we knew, must have occurred elsewhere. So very many poor souls had not survived that night and untold numbers had suffered the most horrific injuries. Always, during those turbulent weeks and months, we lived from day to day in a constant vague fear; never really knowing if the next day would be our last. Aerial warfare - all warfare - is a ghastly and revolting thing. It solves nothing and causes needless, untold misery to thousands of innocent people.

Preciousness of life and the way in which Lady Luck had smiled on our two families, was vividly brought home to me, only a couple of days later. Just before Christmas 1940, while I was checking greenhouse boilers and routinely fire-watching at work, one night, Merseyside suffered another heavy attack. When away from home, quivering ground and the ominous thud of a non-too distant heavy bomb, caused me agonising concern for the family. A feeling of helpless anguish. 'Where had the damnable thing fallen? Were they all safe?" (We'd no 'phone then).

Just before welcome daylight, the 'All-Clear' whined, mournfully through the early morning air and, not far away, across a narrow lane skirting the nursery land, I could see smoke rising and hear the feverish activity of rescue services. Knowing that our shattered glass must await a daytime check, I apprehensively and with frightening images in my mind, hurried over the small plot of ground to where, it was clear, severe damage must have occurred. Small cottage property, adjoining Sandy Lane, had obviously been hit. Drawing closer, I could see, in the pale light of dawn, that walls of two little houses had just disappeared. A strange odour of dust and burning debris wafted towards me through the cold, damp air. Stumbling over a flattened hedge and piles of rubble, I reached several weary, dirty rescuers. "Think we've got 'em all out," one man mumbled, "The place next door was empty - thank God." A large crater at the back of one house told it's own story.

"Are they, are they very badly hurt?" I murmured, rather lamely, fearing the worst.

"One is, I'm afraid, he was at the back; other four not too bad, cuts and bruises, but all very shocked, though. Old man very low."

Cold sweat glistened on the man's forehead, as he spoke to me, his clothes covered in grime and brick dust. "Why on earth would they bomb here," I exclaimed, a little pointlessly, "it's on the outskirts, it's all country, isn't it?"

"Unloadin' t'get back, I s'pose, there was a lot of 'ack , ack last night." the man answered, wearily, "or p'raps that greenhouse glass shone some light up and they thought it was a factory."

"Yer, could be." I whispered, thinking how close the bomb had been to the nursery. A quarter mile further west would have been right on target, middle of our land.

"Well, if there's nothing I can do and you're OK, I'll get off 'ome. I'm dead worried. They're right in the thick of it there!" My voice trembled with suppressed emotion.

"OK mate, and try not t'worry, I hope they're alright -,they prob'ly are," the rescuer tried to reassure me.

Picking my way back across the debris strewn lane I suddenly noticed, a little lower down than my earlier crossing. A push-bike laying close to the ragged hedge. Partially covered by rubble, the bike was near to a small gap in the flattened vegetation. Moving closer, I was horrified to see a trousered leg protruding from beneath the hedge. Just inside the nursery plot, on soft wet grass, I found the body of a young man about my own age. Almost on his back and with one leg bent under him, he lay, with eyes wide open, as if staring at the reddened morning sky.

Swallowing hard, I nervously kneeled beside him and tried the wrist for a pulse; he was stone cold. With no pulse evident, I fumbled in my inside pocket and brought out a leather sided wallet mirror and placed it close to the lad's parted lips. There was just nothing; no sign of life. Except for torn clothing, cuts and a large bruise to the forehead, he seemed to be unhurt. Then I saw it. Dark blood discoloured the grass below the young chap's head. Gently moving the shoulder, I could see a dreadful gaping wound at the back of his skull. I felt sickened. Flying masonry or shrapnel must have caused that frightful injury.

For a long time, in silence, I knelt quietly beside the lad, nervously shivering, my teeth uncontrollably chattering. I felt strangely dizzy and almost wanted to vomit. Sight of that bloody wound and the wide, unearthly open eyes, deeply shocked me. I'd seen the dead before, but not like this. I was destined to witness more such disturbing sights.

Slowly regaining some semblance of control, I tried to straighten the chap's leg and move his arms to a more normal position, but rigor-mortis had quickly set in, no doubt due to the violent and rapid death. This simple and usual effect upon the dead, in itself, upset me as I looked down at his sad, pale young face, the sightless eyes gazing up at me. Still trembling slightly, in the chill morning air, I quietly mumbled something about doing what I could to help. I'm not at all religious but, involuntarily, I put my hands together and mouthed a silent prayer. Putting two fingers on my lips, I leaned forward and placed those fingers gently on the lad's forehead. "God be with you, son, may you rest in peace," whispered, shakily; tears streaming down my cheeks.

To me, it seemed that a faint smile of thanks briefly flickered across those pallid features, as I looked down at his pitiable, twisted body. Though the rescue workers didn't know the youth, it was later discovered that he'd worked at a not too distant factory and was taking a 'short cut' home when death had claimed him. Bad luck lured him to the wrong place, at the wrong time.

Our two families, by a quirk of fate, had come through another hazardous night, but we were extremely worried about Grandma's house, nearer to town. Cycling down, Chris and I found them safe but considerably shaken after an H.E had exploded nearby. Helping to clean and patch up superficial damage in Gran's place, we were shocked, though not surprised, to hear about the widespread destruction of property in adjacent streets with innumerable casualties.

Night time bombing over the City centre had been heavy, we knew, and, as the acrid smell of smoke drifted up from town direction, we guessed that a neighbour's story of massive devastation was probably true. From the fact that Gran's house had nearly been hit, it was obvious that many small local homes were crushed and scores of little people, like us, had lost their lives. The spectacle wasn't hard to visualise and we iust couldn't visit the scene of their private grief. That, Chris and I thought, would be an unforgivable intrusion into those ordinary working folk's lives, at a time of their deepest sadness and despair. (May Hitler and all his German brood rot in Hell.)

While the City streets with large buildings and familiar shops we knew so well, were part of our lives, they seemed less personal; unlike the rows of small houses full of families whose hopes had been for a better future. Fellow Liverpudlians living all around here now weren't really strangers but just good friends we didn't happen to know. To us, they seemed almost like family.

After leaving Gran's, Chris and I cycled down to town. Somehow, it didn't seem so unjustifiable to view the possible damage there. And serious damage there really was. Unimaginable devastation beyond anything we'd ever seen. Long before reaching the heart of town, we could smell the pungent odour of smoke; we could see greyish smuts with burning and unburnt debris, against the darkened sky, floating in the air high above our heads and sensed the chaos that lay ahead! "My God!" Chris shouted to me, as we sped down Leece and Bold streets, "The whole town must be alight." Indeed, it really seemed that Chris was right, for the scene from Central Station was one of conflagration and utter destruction. Fire must have raged for most of the previous night. Very large fire water hoses ran the length of Church and Lord Streets, while service personnel were fighting a losing battle, valiantly trying to quell the fires or minimize damage wherever possible.

Most of the large shops, we'd known so well, were either burning fiercely out of control, burnt out or rapidly starting to collapse as pathetic, blackened shells. Acrid smoke, smuts, dust and floating debris were unbelievable. With reddened eyes, we both coughed and choked.

"Oh, God. Let's get out of 'ere, I've seen enough!" Croaked Chris, "That's terrible, it's the worst thing I've ever seen," she exclaimed bitterly, "Oh, God, Bernie, will it ever end? We'll all die. How much more of this will there be? She cried, despairingly, trying to hold back the tears. "Jesus, I don't know, Chris, I just don't know, German bastards, they are" I exploded, with seething bitterness, reflecting my hatred for the Nazi scum who'd committed this wanton act of destruction. It was difficult to contain my mounting rage.

Turning angrily from the horrific spectacle before us, I leaned my bike against a wall and put my arm round Chris's shoulders. "Look," I said, trying to calm myself. "We'll survive, Chris, luv, I know we will," I tried to reassure her. "We'll someday look back on all this as just a bad dream - a horrible nightmare."

I held her very close as tears flooded her pretty cheeks. "We've a guardian angel, luv," I whispered, "we really'ave. We'll cum through all this, you'll see" I could feel her anguished heart thumping against my breast, as I pressed my lips to her tear-stained cheek.

"I pray to God, you're right, Bernie," Chris sobbed, "but will we all live to see the end of this awful war?"

"Cum on, luv, don't upset y'self," I tried to soothe. "Let's get off 'ome. This is the town, remember, near the docks; we're on the outskirts, we've all got a better chance there, y'know." My comforting words hardly matched my feelings. I hardly knew what to say, what could one say amidst this appalling devastation. I felt just as down, just as scared and fearful for the future as Chris, and my remarks about our guardian angel seemed little more than very wishful thinking. An image of that young lad I'd seen, killed near to the nursery, constantly haunted my mind. He was one of so very many. Perhaps, in one sense, he'd been lucky, he'd died instantly, or so it seemed, a great many had not.

Our terrible sense of foreboding, as we'd stood there in Church Street, appeared to have been well founded for, less than five months later, Merseyside suffered the worst 'Blitzkreig' of the War. 'THE MAY BLITZ' of 1941.

Lurking at the back of all our minds - as Merseyside's War 'hotted up' - was the knowledge that we had little real protection from air raids! Pa reinforced a space under the stairs and fitted wooden shutters to the rear windows of the house to afford some shelter; rather 'puny' against the possible attacks! Many people, having gardens, were provided with Anderson shelters; do-it-yourself corrugated iron structures easily erected a bit below ground, and covered with soil. This was a dubious and often water-logged shelter providing some protection, I suppose, from flying shrapnel.

Our street had several brick built, concrete roofed affairs constructed on the road. Small, and to me claustrophobic, these places could be a real hazard at times, as was proved by the disaster which occurred at Durning Road Junior Technical School. 'Jerry' dropped a land-mine close to the shelter, early one November morning, 1940, and part of the roof collapsed, killing about 160 poor souls. Great devastation and severe loss of life also occurred when a similar bomb dropped on Fern Grove (off Lodge Lane) at about the same time.

Land-mines, used in the early part of the War, were one of the numerous 'terror weapons' dreamed up by that monstrous little, evil German bastard, Hitler, to drop onto innocent civilians. The device, size of a pillar-box, contained about 700 lbs of high explosive and was dropped by parachute so that it would not penetrate the earth but would explode just above or at ground level. The Nazi German's ruthless purpose was to cause as much possible carnage over the widest possible area. To kill, maim and mutilate as many innocent people as possible. That was the Nazi German's 'friendly message' to all who stood in their way. They were, indeed, a very friendly people.

Christmas during our childhood, as I've said, was a rather frugal, low key affair but times had gradually improved. Now, in 1940, we seemed to be back to 'square one.' Most things were rationed, times were getting harder and a great deal more frightening than anything we'd ever known. Chris, Kate, I myself and the families had no option but to do the best we could for Christmas. All of us tried our level best to be as cheerful as possible under nerve racking conditions, hard to describe.

Even with all the raids we'd suffered, in the north, London had been subjected to far worse. Incendiaries, in early September, had set London ablaze and, on September 15th, a huge air attack, by the Luftwaffe (German Air Force) hoping to 'soften up' our defences prior to a possible invasion was fearlessly beaten back by the so called FEW, *great* R.A.F lads, who actually 'downed' 56 Nazi planes. Our well developed RADAR system undoubtedly helped in this great success.

This *Battle of Britain* achievement in our skies proved to be a 'turning point' in the air warfare, although many more raids were still yet to come. Before New Year, December 29th, hundreds of incendiaries caused about 1500 fires all over battered London. Amazingly, St. Paul's Cathedral escaped damage, although the blazing inferno could be seen over sixty miles away.

Invasion of Britain by the German hordes had been a possibility for some time and although the Hun's plan, 'Operation Sealion' (sea borne invasion of Britain), had been postponed indefinitely, unbeknown to us the threat of sea-borne landings and visions of 'jack-booted thugs' crossing the Channel to these

Islands, was still very real to all of us in Britain. A brutal occupation, as already seen in Europe, would undoubtedly be established here if an invasion was to take place.

Despite the 'Bulldog' spirit, fearful insecurity gave rise to a degree of despondency and no-one felt safe, or at all certain that we'd eventually win the War. The future did, indeed, seem more than bleak.

In fact Christmas 1940 was, to us, the gloomiest we could ever remember. However, in spite of the country's prospects and all the doom and gloom, we as Liverpudlians always do, tried desperately to hang on to a bit of humour; a bit of faith and hope to face an uncertain future, and even toasted the New Year with a wish and prayer for the defeat of Nazi Germany, a speedy end to the ghastly War and a longed for peaceful tomorrow.

Yes, unbelievably, 'The Three Musketeers.' The Three Kids from old Liverpool, along with all the rest of our mates, although very, very down, were not yet, by any means, out.

CHAPTER 4

The Nightmares recede
A glimpse of happier times ahead

One means of escape from a depressing situation - if only for a couple of hours - was a visit to the to the 'pictures' and Chris, Kate and I tried the 'remedy' whenever possible

'All places of public assembly' - as the Government so succinctly put it - were closed at the outbreak of War but, because of the public outcry during the 'phoney war,' theatres and cinemas were soon reopened, life was bad enough as it was. A few of the many films, we three remember, were the Andy Hardy series - with Mickey Rooney and Lewis Stone, Laurel and Hardy's 'Flying Deuces,' 'The Cat and the Canary' with Bob Hope and Paulette Goddard and numerous Boris Karloff pictures which, to me, were always good for a laugh. These supposedly 'creepy' dramas were, by today's standards, a laugh-a-minute. I realise, too, that I've got a perverted sense of humour.

Still on films, I remember Chris, while scanning the *Liverpool Echo* cinema index, saying to Kate, "Oh, look, we three'll have to see this."

"What's that?" asked Kate, with mild curiosity.

"Yes, what's so great, that's tickled your fancy?" I added. Chris grinned wickedly at Kate and answered, "Deanna Durbin - no less."

"Oh, great," Kate cut in, enthusiastically.

"In," Chris continued, glancing at Kate with a knowing smile, "Three Smart Girls!". Kate, looking at me, burst out laughing. "Well!" I cried, with a grin, "What the heck y'lookin' at me for, as if I didn't know."

"Now, look, just put that old hat of y'ma's on and you'll really look the part," Chris chortled.

"Oh, will I now, y'don't say," I retorted, hitting Chris with the newspaper.

"I'm not goin' out with him in that" exploded Kate, "He'd look like Charlie's Aunt and we'd look a right set of 'twirps" We all collapsed laughing at the idea of me 'dolled up as a bird.' It's a jolly good job we could laugh about something. At least, it raised our flagging spirits.

Even at work - perhaps due to working in the great outdoors - incidents occurred which often raised a laugh. As sometimes happens, an innocent victim, in this case John, the foreman, was at the receiving end of this unfortunate yet amusing mishap. From time to time, younger members of staff were detailed to barrow down loads of anthracite - from a huge stock-pile - to feed the two large 'Robin Hood' boilers which heated a number of glass houses.

In front of the potting shed bench, a large hole - covered by an iron plate - provided access to the coal bunker. When away for a load of coal, one fixed a wooden bar, at waist height, across the door entrance to warn anyone that the hole was uncovered. Having tipped a coal-load down and shifted the wheelbarrow, I was interrupted by a chap looking for young June.

Turning and moving a few feet to the greenhouse, I pointed her out to our visitor. Now then, unbeknown to me, in those few seconds when my back was turned, John trotted down from the stores with a very large bag of spagnum moss clutched in his arms, en route to the potting bench. Need I say more. Not hearing a sound, I re-entered the shed to find John, his face considerably redder than usual, leaning against the bench, puffing and blowing.

"Are you alright, what's happened? "I asked, with some trepidation, secretly realising John's misfortune. Really sorry but also amused, I tried desperately not to smirk.

"Been down that bloody hole, haven't I. Why the hell didn't y'cover it for God's sake?" As the bunker was nearly full, John only dropped about two feet onto the coal. With little more than bruises and a great loss of dignity, he was reasonably alright. My explanation and profuse apologies did little to assuage his wrath because, I suspect, he detected the barely concealed amusement behind my apparent concern for his welfare. Mind you, weeks later, we both laughed about it - after he 'd called me a few choice names.

Incidentally, I never really lived down my attempt to knock off the foreman, as Chris and the gang so eloquently put it! Ben, of course, said I'd tried to do what Hitler's bombs had failed to accomplish. But, then, he would, wouldn't he?

Early 'forty one's quieter mood, due to the lull in German air activity, changed dramatically towards the end of April. For the whole of May, right through to about mid June, Merseyside suffered the worst bombing of the War. Later dubbed The May Blitz. Hardly a night passed without 'moaning minnie' - air raid warnings - wailing out across the town, with its ominous message of impending disaster. During those terrible five or six weeks, I'm sure that most people were resigned to fatalistic acceptance of the ghastly situation. There was really no escape; if one's name was on a bomb, that was it. you were dead or worse, frightfully injured.

Shelters provided protection from flying shrapnel and debris; that's all. For complete safety, one needed to be ten feet or so underground. The elite and those with money could make sure of the best. The little people of Merseyside didn't enjoy such luxury. The little people never do. Innocent majorities always suffer most in war.

'Screaming,' terror bombs, dropped by German Nazi scum, caused untold pain and misery to thousands of inoffensive people all over Britain. Later, random V1 and V2 terror bombs, designed by conscienceless, evil Nazi bastards, were rained down on southern England to kill and maim as many civilians as possible. The Nazis really were a wonderful Master Race. Not the Salt of the Earth; just the Scum of the Earth.

One very frightening May night started, like many others, with the usual early, wailing, siren warning. In our little terrace house, Kate, myself, Ma and Pa were huddled together in our 'refuge' room - at the back - with its wooden shuttered window and minimum furniture. A large bed was pushed into one corner while a camp bed fitted an alcove by the fire. Dozing on a downstairs bed or huddled together under the reinforced stairs, seemed a safer option than being in an upstairs bedroom. It wasn't, of course, but we hoped to God, it was.

After another hard workday, Pa lay in a fitful slumber on the bed - fully dressed, ready for any emergency - while we sat around trying to make whispered conversation and constantly listening to distant 'ack-ack' (anti-aircraft fire), as Goering's droning Luftwaffe bombers winged their way up from the Channel coast. German planes, flying high, seemed to emit a strange, pulsating and unmistakable sound, now so very familiar.

Pa, asleep but dressed in warden's gear, stirred nervously as the well remembered sounds drifted into his conscious mind. Reluctantly, I was about to wake him from an uneasy sleep, when a distant bomb fell, frighteningly vibrating the sash window and shutters.

"God - that wasn't far away". Hardly had the words passed my lips, when an H.E dropped very, very close. The whole place seemed to lift and shake as the shutters rattled violently, but the window held. Pa, still half asleep, sat up involuntarily, his face drained white.

"What the hell ---------?" Then, immediately fully awake and realising the situation, he shouted.

"Quick, you two, under the stairs! Bernie, outside, we've

got to get outside". I was already dragging on my coat and siezed my gas mask. Ma, her face deathly pale, glanced at Pa, "Wait! Your mask and tin hat, you've no hat. Oh, for God's sake, hang on till they've passed". Before Ma could utter another word, a third bomb exploded.

"God! That's on top of us. Don't go now Bernie". Kate cried, clinging to my arm in terror, "You'll be killed, both of you. Oh, God! don't go, Bernie," she sobbed, "They're right over us".

"No, they've passed, Kate, luv, when y'can hear the 'thud' close to," y'know they've moved away, We've got to go, Kate; there's poor beggars dyin' out there. I'm scared, too, Kate, but they're dyin' - they need help." I tried to keep a steady voice, but I was cold with fear. "I know," Kate whispered, through her tears, "but, be careful, both of you" she said, regaining some composure. During a slight lull, following the heavy bombing we prepared to leave. "They're definitely movin' away, now," I tried to reassure Ma and Kate. Pa, grim faced, glanced quickly at me; we both knew that didn't mean a thing. Bombs could easily miss but many more could be on the way.

Muffled in heavy coats, against cold night air, Pa and I left the house, with dry throats and pounding hearts, peering fearfully into that frightening void above our heads, whilst glimpsing mental images of what might be awaiting us out there in the dark. Searchlights, thin pencils of light, wandered across the heavens pin-pointing enemy craft, while occasional 'ack-ack' shells were visible bursting against the distant night sky. All the time, we could hear that peculiar, unearthly drone of German planes, thousands of feet above our heads, preparing to drop more misery and death anywhere, at any moment.

Many incendiaries lay in the roads and on a school playground, but some had found a target and were being frantically tackled as we made our way, amidst the 'clump clump' of H.E's un-nervingly close, towards a blaze just a couple of streets away. The scene, when we arrived, was one of the usual devastation of these dreadful times. Several houses had disappeared while those on either side seemed, in a grotesque way, to be structurally clinging to life, much like the poor human souls trapped amidst the smouldering rubble. With fire quelled, Wardens and the rest of us carefully prodded and moved masses of debris, mostly with our bare hands, to rescue the living, badly injured, or, sadly, to recover the dead. With neighbours' information and help, we continued our feverish, frightening search for those still missing. Personal fear from the ever present threat of falling brickwork, masonry and further raids, quickly vanished from our thoughts. Nothing concentrates the mind so swiftly as the vivid realisation that someone's life may depend on one's own efforts to get them out of this nightmare situation. Thoughts quickly focus sharply on the rescue, to the exclusion of everything else! When extricating badly injured casualties, however, we quickly learned to curb any emotional involvement. It plays havoc with the nerves and greatly impedes one's ability to make a rapid and successful rescue. War speedily teaches one many things, in many different ways. Just this one night coping with some horrendous injuries, left us both sickened, deeply shocked and spiritually scarred. Everyone felt the same, I suppose, but we all carried on, we just had to.

One event, less frightening but bizarre and very sad, remains in my mind. A house, to the left of the main devastation, still retained its stairs and wall while the bedroom had almost collapsed into the living room below. Hanging drunkenly, from one hinge, the bedroom door swung gently against the wall. Suddenly, a young girl, carrying a lighted candle and dressed only in her nightdress, appeared in the doorway, standing on what remained of the landing. Grotesquely, she raised the candle and was calling into the shattered room. Someone shouted from the street, "Don't move, don't move - we'll get you out!" Maybe stunned by the explosion or deafened, she didn't make any sign

ONE OF MANY HEART RENDING INCIDENTS –
– LIVERPOOL'S MAY 'BLITZ' 1941 –

and just stood gazing into the darkened space, where the room had once been.

Realising that scattered debris made quick use of a ladder impossible, a young Warden, close to the smashed front door, made a sudden dash up the precarious staircase, grabbed the girl, pulling her close to the wall, then stumbled with her down to the hallway. Another Warden, carrying a bright electric torch, leapt forward to assist and prevent them falling to the floor. Seconds after the courageous rescue, staircase and landing, weakened by the extra weight of a man, just collapsed. Still dazed, incoherent and scratched, the girl appeared to be otherwise unhurt but quickly passed out and was taken for medical care. Her grandfather had been in the bedroom, now shattered, when the bomb had fallen and was, very sadly, amongst the dead.

Nearly every night, right through May and into early June, this frightening situation was the pattern of Liverpool's life, to a greater or lesser extent. Many innocent civilians were killed or maimed for no other reason than that they happened to be in the wrong place at the wrong time. Scars to body, heart and mind of the good folks in Liverpool during that terrible 'May Blitz' were, unfortunately, only part of the overall pattern of death and destruction, up and down the country. Towns like Manchester, Coventry, Plymouth, London, of course and many more, suffered even worse carnage in heavy air attacks. Only the ordinary folk everywhere, who lived through the trauma and saw the utter devastation of their towns and cities, can really comprehend the full horror of total War.

After Liverpool's ghastly experiences of May 'forty one, our two families very slowly returned to a life with some semblance of normality. It was, however, 1942 before the last 'All Clear' sounded and, even then - although we weren't aware of it - another three years of war still lay ahead.

By mid '42, having achieved good school results, our dear Kate left home for the first time.

Accepted as a student nurse, by the hospital Training School, she was to stay at the nearby Nurses' Home. After twelve months away she would be entitled to three weeks leave! Being so very close, since we were kids together, I was going to miss Kate dreadfully and I knew she felt the same about leaving home. Packing all finished, very tearful goodbyes proceeded her departure as we all realised that twelve months seemed an awfully long time.

"I'm not going to Africa, Bernie," she murmured, trying her best to smile, "and I'll write, I'll keep in touch, all the time, honest".

Holding back the tears, I joked, "You see y'do now. Oh, and by the way, watch out for those young doctors chasing y'round the wards".

"You've got a one track mind, you," she giggled and. threw her arms round my neck, hugging me tightly. Ma came in from the hall, "Taxi's here, luv. You sure you've got everything now, luv?" she asked.

"You take y'time, Kate, to say y'cheerios, and I'll take all these bits out to the cab," I said, realising that Ma wanted a few final private words with Kate before she left. Dear Kate was only seventeen and her leaving home - if only for a spell - was an emotional jolt for both of them. Girls weren't quite as sophisticated in the 'forties'.

The letter received from Kate, a couple of days later, was full of reassurances and mild enthusiasm concerning the hospital and her little room in the Nurses Home. Classes would start, she said, on Monday and she might commence some practical training in Ward 2 under Senior Staff Nurse Hicks. I couldn't help wondering if poor Kate's enthusiasm would, hold once she became a student nurse under Senior Staff Nurse Hicks. However, knowing Kate's grit and determination, I felt confident that she wouldn't be easily deterred, by anything or anyone. She had a positive approach to most problems and was very keen to

KATE
BERNIE
CHRIS
THE TEEN-AGE 'TRIO'
(EARLY-1942)
(V.L.EDWARDS)

become a good nurse. Kate, too, was a survivor - in every sense of the word - like the rest of us. We'd always had to be.

Soon after Kate settled in at the hospital, news in her next letter confirmed that she was beginning to adjust very nicely to the job and strange new environment. Always a quick learner, she enjoyed the classes and, although Senior Staff Nurse Hicks, who'd been there a long time, was a stickler for efficiency, Kate admired the way in which she ran the Ward with effortless smoothness, under the supervision of the Ward Sister. Being keen to progress and do her best, Kate seemed to think that her work, so far, had satisfied the eagle eye of Staff Nurse Hicks. Kate's own words, at the end of her letter were, to me, all important. 'I know I'll be happy here'.

In the weeks that followed, Kate's cheery presence was sadly missed at home and Chris felt lonely too; they were such very good friends. Neither Chris nor I had a 'phone and it was sometimes difficult to contact Kate by public line. Letters, our principal means of communication, were eagerly awaited and very quickly read again and again.

In our free time Chris and I - being engaged - often wandered round 'eyeing' houses for sale and rent. We couldn't afford one, of course, but we liked to just look and dream. Wide eyed we'd both sometimes peer through large show room, windows at lovely little run-about cars, pointing out the qualities of each. Turning, we'd walk away, arm in arm, laughing at our happy fantasies.

"Wouldn't it be great to win the Pools, Bernie? Everything we've ever wanted, just like that," Chris chuckled.

"That's about the only ruddy way we'll get a little 'chariot' now," I answered, regretfully. "Mind you, I could do a lot more overtime or," I continued with a wicked grin, "you could take on a well, nice sort-of high paid modelling job, you know." I quickly pulled my arm away from Chris and held it up, protectively, in front of my face. Chris quickly belted me with her handbag.

"Oh, could I? And what exactly do y'mean by that? - as if I didn't know." She belted me again and burst out laughing. I grabbed her, pinning her arms, and kissed her hard on the lips.

"We'll get the 'ready' someday, kid," I cried, "You'll see and that's a promise." A middle aged couple, passing, laughed and the man called over, "Taint so easy, these days, son, but we wish you luck."

Chris, her face crimson, shouted back, "Thanks, we'll need it. He's always full of 'pipe dreams' this lad." The lady, now some way along the pavement, called, "Well, good on 'im, and why not? They can cum true, y'know, luv."

We weren't, by any means, the only young folks trying to cope with wartime life. For many workers in munition and other factories, pay and conditions didn't seem so good. Repetitive, monotonous jobs in unhealthy environments and long working hours, wasn't exactly a picnic. With my heart condition, which wasn't too bad, the, more or less outdoor life at the nursery was far healthier, even if the pay was less. Also, in the early part of the war, factories had been 'sitting' targets for the German Luftwaffe. Now, however, at the end of '42, air raids had eased off - in the North, anyway.

Although money was still 'tight,' some people, no doubt because of war's uncertainty adopted an 'eat-drink and be-merry' attitude and often spent, without much thought, the extra cash they could earn from, suddenly available, wartime jobs. Hoping that times and conditions would improve, Chris and I tried to save for a better future life together. I think we did the right thing.

Early on in the War, my Dad's financial prospects had, thankfully, improved when he managed to land a foreman's job on a Government contract. Regular, constant work, after the heartaches of the twenties and thirties, really put a spring back in his step. It's surprising what regular employment can do for a man's ego. Pa was a jolly good tradesman and, despite his age and the War, he looked younger and felt happy in the knowledge that he was, at last, bringing home a reasonable, regular weekly wage. I can see Ma's face now, when Pa, after his first big overtime week, threw an unopened wage packet on the table in front of her. "How's that Ma" he said with pride, grinning at both of us. Remembering all the hard times - with hardly two pennies to rub together - there were tears in her eyes as she looked at the bulging wage envelope.

"It's - it's great, luv, it really is," she whispered, shakily. "Hope it lasts. Wish the times were better, though, don't you? Sorry, luv, I didn't mean to be pessimistic, this is a great start; it'll help us out no end." Her face suddenly lit up."Course things'll get better,wont they? I'm being an old misery guts, aren't I," She went over and kissed my Pa and they both hugged one another.

"That's more like my gel," Pa laughed, "We'll cum out on top yet, Ma, by God, we will".

One cold evening in early December 'forty two, Chris walked into our house, devoid of her usual jaunty style, and was obviously very upset. Alarmed, I jumped up from my fireside chair and grasped her arm, "Chris, luv, whatever's the matter?" Quickly, she blurted out, "Mum's ill, Bernie."

"God! I've never seen y'like this, what's happened?"

"Mum she's". Chris broke off, bit her lip and her eyes filled with tears,"There's a lump in her breast, Bernie". Immediately, morbid thoughts shot through my mind. Deeply shocked, I knew what it **might** be. Quickly gathering my wits, I said, "Here, Chris, sit down. Look, it might not be so bad. How long has she had this thing? I mean, has she seen the 'quack'?" Chris seldom cried, but now tears flooded down her cheeks as she whispered, "We didn't know she'd been. She's got to go for some test. Oh, God, she's got cancer, Bernie." Chris's whole body shook as she sobbed. Quickly, I sat beside her and held her very close.

"Chris, luv, it may not be. The test'll be a biopsy, it could show she's alright. Not all these things are cancer, y'know."

"How d'you know? Who said?" she murmured, looking up at me with so much fear in her lovely eyes. It was just possible that the test could be negative, but I didn't want to raise false hopes. "Oh, I saw it in a paper, one of those doctor's columns, y'know; doctor's answers to questions. When's your mum got to go for the test?"

"On Thursday," Chris replied and then added quietly, hoping for the right answer, "D'you really think it's somethin' else, Bernie?"

I desperately wanted to say yes, but I couldn't in case my hopes were unfounded. "I hope so, luv, if it's just benign, as they call it, the doc'll give her treatment and she could be out in no time, Chris."

"What'll they have t'do? I mean, will they have to - to cut it out." she said fearfully, with, no doubt, frightening mental images flashing through her mind.

"Look, Chris, don't get yourself all worked up. We'll go with her and make sure she's OK. She's pretty tough, y'Mum, but she needs a lot of our support, right now. Just don't let her think you're scared. Try and act normally to help her cope with it."

"I know she's awful worried, but she keeps quiet for our sakes. We've said nothing to upset her, Bernie, honest we 'aven't."

"Well, no, course not, I didn't think y'had, really. Look, I've been thinking, p'raps if you and your Ma went alone to the hospital, she'd feel calmer and then Ma and I can drop in later to hear the test result. If - God-forbid - the test is positive, then Ma'll be there to have a quiet word with y'mum. The doctor'd understand. Ma's cousin had the same thing, y'know, Chris."

The radical surgery of mastectomy was a fearsome thing for any woman and my Ma, knowing the full implications and being about the same age as Chris's mum, felt she might give a little comfort and reassurance, should the need arise.

As arranged, when the time arrived, we met Chris in the hospital waiting room and sat there, nervously awaiting the biopsy result. The minutes seemed like hours. All our hearts, quite literally, missed a beat when, with a slight smile, a smart young nurse appeared and whispered that laboratory tests indicated a small benign tumour only, was present in the left breast.

A simple operation was all that would be required, with little or no disfigurement and every possibility of a good and speedy recovery. Bursting into tears, from pent up emotion, Chris wept with nervous relief. "There's no cancer, then? She'll be alright?" Chris asked, through her tears. "Of course she will, dear." the nurse comforted. "Your mother will be fine in a few days really. After the doctor has performed the small, straightforward operation, you'll soon be able to speak to her and put your mind at rest. Now, don't worry, dear, she'll be fine." About to move away, the nurse smiled and said, "You could do with a nice cup of tea, luv, I'll have one sent over; it'll calm you down."

"Oh, yes, nurse, that'd be luvly, thanks." Chris murmured, regaining some composure. Ma smiled, approvingly, "Thanks nurse, you're very kind. She needs a good strong 'cuppa'."

Wiping her eyes, Chris relaxed a little and waited quietly for the comforting tea. Optimistic news was great but, I could see, shadowy doubts still lingered in Chris's mind. Gently I kissed her cheek,"Y'Mum'll be fine, luv,"I whispered, warmly embracing her. "I hope so, Bernie, oh, I hope so."

Facing up to a simple, though possibly life threatening medical condition in a loved one, seemed to be more distressing to us than many a trauma we'd experienced during this long and dreary War. Happily, Chris's mum made a reasonably rapid recovery - both physical and mental -from her alarming disorder, and we all breathed deep sighs of greatful relief.

Our Kate, naturally upset over the news, now assured us, after a word with Nurse Hicks, at the Teaching Hospital, that Chris's mother was unlikely to suffer any further problems. From her frequent letters, it seemed that Kate was making quite good progress in her chosen profession. So far, she had worked in two wards and was now very busy in a third. Incidentally, Staff Nurse Hicks wasn't the 'ogre' she was said to be, and Kate's genuine interest and willingness to learn resulted in a strict but very friendly atmosphere in the Ward.

My very close bond with Kate and the details she revealed to me later, enable me to recount experiences from her very personal viewpoint; Kate's very own thoughts, hopes and fears during her long absence from home.

Dermatology was, Kate knew, an important part of medicine but her 'stint' on the ward dealing with skin complaints wasn't particularly pleasant. Interesting and informative though it might be, spreading evil smelling ointments on various anatomical parts of, sometimes, very irritable patients, left a lot to be desired. Poor Kate could smell the aroma well before she arrived for duty. Ventilation didn't seem to prevent the assault on her nostrils.

In the very different environment of Ward 3, Kate's close encounter with patients, of great strength of spirit, left a lasting impression on her mind. Very many, although not all in the Ward, had congenital bone deformaties which, in the outside world, had made them objects of curiosity, pity and even amusement. Here, in a friendly atmosphere, they mixed and were equals. Encouraging one another, they talked amongst themselves and to the nurses without shyness or embarrassment. Hope of improvement or a cure burned in all their hearts and minds and, always, they tried. God knows, they tried. Crippled in body they might be, but their brains were fully alert and completely untrammelled.

Pain, and sometimes humiliation, was nothing new to many but they took it in their stride, without the irritability often shown by we lesser mortals to more minor complaints. Gazing across the Ward, Kate couldn't help but admire the strength and fortitude of these wonderful people. They really put us all to shame; we able bodied folk.

Being fairly large, Ward 3 provided care for quite a few bone fracture cases and the like, apart from the congenitally deformed patients. Work on the Ward, could be very exhausting at times and busy orderlies were not always available to lend a hand in, perhaps, lifting a patient. Nurses were not supposed to lift anyone unaided, but they frequently did. Assisting someone from bed to a wheelchair could be quite a task for a slimly built girl. Despite the hard work, Kate enjoyed her duties on Ward 3, particularly helping the appreciative congenital patients, whom she would always remember with great affection.

With examinations out of the way, Kate soon realised that her first full year of training would, in a week or two, be completed and she'd be off home for a glorious three weeks leave. Training classes and the general hurly-burly of hospital life made Kate feel that time had just flown and yet, especially in the early months, she'd been so home-sick that she'd just wanted to cry. She really missed home a lot, but Kate knew that to dwell on the matter too much would affect her work and her future career. All the same, the very nearness of her holiday made her 'bubbly' with excitement and she found herself day-dreaming on the Ward. Ma, Pa, Bernie and Chris; she pictured them all in her mind's eye and wondered if they'd changed much in twelve months, and if they'd think she had. There'd been letters, of course, but she still wondered how they'd really fared over this long, last year of 1943. Warm tears filled her eyes, she was terribly home-sick again. "Nurse, nurse." Someone needed her; she came back to earth with a bump to resume her vital duties. 'It isn't time yet, Kate, get a grip, gel," she murmured to herself. The Nursing Supervisor would contact her at the appropriate time; she must curb her growing excitement and be patient.

Meanwhile, we at home missed Kate a very great deal but, except from her letters, we couldn't really know how much she longed for home. We guessed she did; but it was obvious, from her writing, that she was deeply committed to nursing and determined to succeed in the profession, even if it meant being away from home for another four years.

According to her last letter, Kate would be home on 14th September, which would give us all time to collect together the necessary items for a home-coming party. As everything was now rationed, we'd have to beg, borrow or 'fiddle' things for the event, and do the very best we could. Ma and Chris's mum were experts at improvisation - they'd always had to be - and managed to 'rustle up' and create, as if by magic, not only a party atmosphere but an assortment of table delicacies fit for a queen.

I still tended to regard Kate as my lovable, young kid sister but now realised that she'd grown up very quickly. Everyone wanted her first leave to be a happy, memorable occasion and an item of news, we knew she'd be pleased to hear, was that Chris and I planned to marry next Spring, It was to be hoped that Kate could 'wangle' a couple of days to attend the wedding as a bridesmaid! She and young June, from work, would look lovely in the part; there was little doubt of that.

Family and friends, delighted to welcome our Kate back home after so long and ready with all the local gossip, gathered at our place on the day of Kate's arrival. A large pink paper banner, bearing the words *Welcome Home Kate*, festooned the wall above the decorated fireplace mantelshelf in the parlour, while a well set out table groaned under its appetizing load. Crammed into the small front sitting room, a dozen of us prepared to spring the party surprise on my unsuspecting kid sister.

Hearing the taxi arrive, Ma dashed to the door and, after a very warm, affectionate mother and daughter embrace, whisked Kate quickly into the parlour for an uproariously, boisterous welcome from the 'gang'. Flabbergasted, Kate delightedly shouted to everyone, before I grabbed her for a really big kiss, our first embrace for twelve long months.

"Jes. it's been a long time. I've missed y'Kate." I cried, tearfully, "We've all missed you. Oh, God, it's good t'see you, kid."

Kate, her face flushed red, exclaimed, above the din of noisy conversation, "Me too, Bernie, me too." Tears streamed down her face as she squeezed me tightly and pressed her cheek close to mine. "I've missed home and all of you so much, Bernie," she whispered, sorrowfully.

"Hey, you two, this is an 'appy get together, what's all those tears?" Pa jovially shouted across. Kate quickly ran over and flung both arms round his neck, "Sorry, Dad, I've missed you a lot, I really 'ave!" Pa lifted Kate off her feet, twirling her round as he kissed her."I know gel, I know. Y'look great. Your Ma and me are always thinkin' about you, Kate. We thought you'd be Matron, by now. Y'know, running the hospital," he joked.

Everyone heard Pa's remark and laughingly cheered.

"Take no notice, Kate," called Chris. "When you are Matron, they'll all be queuing up for a bed."

Young June came over and warmly embraced Kate, "Gosh, I'm glad t'see you, Kate," she said, with a look of beaming admiration. "I'd luv to be a nurse, y'know, but isn't it a bit scarey, Kate? I mean, didn't you faint when you saw an operation?" she questioned, apprehensively. Poor Kate looked a little embarrassed. "Well, actually, I haven't seen one yet," she whispered apologetically.

"For goodness sake," laughed John, "don't y'think she's had enough of hospitals, for now. Give the gel a sherry and put a record on the gram. Come on nurse. I mean, Kate, give us a kiss," he laughed, "your Dad's just 'ad one."

Kate, giggling, grabbed John in a warm embrace and gave him a real 'plonker.' More kisses and hugs continued all round, before Kate managed to settle down with a sherry and biscuit.

In happy party mood, Kate listened to and enjoyed all the last twelve months, news and local gossip, as appetizing aromas drifted in from the kitchen. Helped by Chris and her mum, Ma had prepared a tempting chicken dinner, with all the trimmings. A drop of wine greatly enhanced the meal as we all 'tucked' in and, with pudding and innumerable sweetmeats to follow, everyone really enjoyed a hearty 'feast.' The ladies had, bless their hearts, produced a wonderful meal, considering the very difficult and frustrating wartime conditions.

After the satisfying repast, with jovial conversation very much in full flow round the dinner table, Chris suddenly piped up, "Well, our Kate, d'you like the surprise party in your honour?"

"Yes, come on nurse, give us a few words," John exclaimed, sitting back and raising his glass, "Speech," somebody giggled.

"Speech! Y'joking," Kate laughed. "But, yes, I really think the party's great and it's marvellous that you all made the effort. I'd like to thank Ma, Pa, Chris and her mum for all their hard work to make it possible. Gosh, it's luvly to see you all, you've really made my day. Thanks gang," Kate flushed with happiness and took a 'swig' of sherry, as everybody clapped.

"Jolly good, Kate," John praised, "we've all missed your cheery face, we really have. Pa jumped up on his feet, "D'you know, folks, it's just so great to see our little gel home again - if it is only for a couple of weeks - and I hope she'll be back next May for the Wedding. Kate's the best daughter a man could 'ave and I know she'll make a smashin' nurse," Pa raised his glass,

"I give you all a toast - to Our Kate" Everyone lifted their glass, "To Kate, to Kate!" came the chorus and I leaned across to kiss her cheek. A little embarrassed, Kate giggled, "Thanks again, gang, but I think we ought to be toasting Chris and Bernie, who'll soon be getting married!"

"Hear 'ear," they all shouted; quickly turning their attentions to Chris as Kate laughingly added, "And then, I might become an auntie, mightn't I?" She glanced knowingly at Chris.

"Oh, aye, we're 'aving six - three of each!" Chris nudged me, "Aren't we, darling?" she tittered.

"Hey, steady on, Chris." I retorted, with feigned concern, "who the heck's goin' t'keep that lot?"

"Well, y'know, Bernie," Ma cut in, "your gran' had seven - eight, really; one died."

"Holy smoke," Andy cried, "Fancy having eight kids!"

"They all had big families in those days."said Pa, "My mother 'ad six; some 'ad ten or twelve."

"My God." Exploded John, you could start your own football team."

"Wonder how on earth they all got fed?" Questioned June, incredulously.

"That's a good question, gel" Pa replied, sadly, "the answer is sometimes they didn't, they went 'ungry."

"Eh, knock it off, Pa, " Ma laughingly chided, "this is a party, not a ruddy funeral. 'Ere, June, p'raps you'd like a bit more trifle."

"No thanks, really, I've done well," June smirked, " not another bite."

A round of laughs followed when Pa 'pulled bacon' at Ma and nearly dropped his 'fag' in the jelly. With all the old jokes, loads of street gossip, as much 'tipple' and as many cigarettes as were available, Kate's first afternoon and evening at home went with a swing and almost felt like old times. It may have been wartime, but that hadn't spoilt the party atmosphere and didn't prevent one or two of us from becoming a shade 'tipsy,' by late in the evening.

During the next couple of weeks or so, when Kate wasn't enjoying a lie in or being treated to a well earned breakfast in bed, she was off out on her own or with Chris and me and even managed to visit our nursery, where she and young June had a brief chat concerning the bridesmaids dresses which Ma had mentioned she'd got in mind for the pair of them at our wedding.

Kate's short holiday enabled her and Ma to discuss and settle details concerning the wedding gowns and Mum made a start on the work. A lot could be done while Kate was home and then Ma intended checking the fit, and any alterations required, when visiting Kate shortly before the actual wedding. Having seen much of our mam's previous work, I knew that the dresses she'd make for my Chris, Kate and young June would be just perfect. After all, she was an expert in the so called *Rag Trade*!

I must admire the interest and effort displayed by women on and for these notable occasions, compared with the apparent nonchalant attitude of we mere men. Perhaps there is something in the notion that men are less interested in - or, maybe, just scared to death of wedding preparations and, possibly, not so romantic as women. Anyway, after Chris and I fixed a marriage date, all of our women folk were then determined to ensure that the *Big Event* would be a great success and a really romantic Day to remember. God bless'm. We were both looking forward to a wonderful wedding!

CHAPTER 5

Feverish Activity - The Big Day Arrives

Her three week holiday, seemingly, gone in a flash, Kate now found herself back at the hospital. Walking to the entrance, she felt far less apprehensive now than when taking the same rather nervous steps only twelve months before. This was her world now; the feel and atmosphere of the place attracted her. Kate knew that she really belonged. Nursing was her vocation; the thing she had to do.

Reporting to the Training School office, Kate discovered that her duty, tomorrow, would be in the Emergency Ward. A day and night hive of activity, for the most part this large ward, with small operating and recovery rooms, dealt with patients from all walks of life; victims of accident, violence, attempted suicide and even murder.

Until now, many wartime casualties had been brought here but, after emergency treatment, they were transferred to other parts of the hospital. The number of such patients admitted had now greatly reduced, which did help to lessen the work-load. Thinking, excitedly, of the valuable experience she might gain working in this usually busy environment, Kate was very pleased to have been picked for Emergency Ward duty.

Leading up to the Christmas period and beyond, life was fairly hectic in the E.W. Working mostly in the main ward, Kate's duties took her, sometimes, to a large adjoining ward reserved for short stay or overnight patients. Kate's diligence and deep sense of concern for those in her care, gave little time for daydreams about friends and loved ones she'd left behind at home. Still, back in the small room, she'd managed to retain at the nurses home, Kate was always able to unwind, relax and then, having gathered her thoughts, sit down and happily pen a couple of pages to the family.

In all her qualifying years, Kate never forgot home and her letters were always interesting and very sincere. Her roots were very important to Kate and the friendly people of Liverpool were never far from her thoughts.

By early 1944 life was becoming increasingly busy for all of us at home. With our wedding planned for May 20th, everything we hoped to do before that date made time a rapidly dwindling commodity. Ma and Pa had agreed to let Chris and me live at home after our marriage. The middle bedroom and small back dining room would provide a nice little private abode until, later on, we might find a small place of our own. Decorating the two rooms, furnishing the, now empty, bedroom and partly refurnishing the living room, took up a lot of our spare time. A new, low priced bedroom suite was bought while other second-hand items had been promised by well-wishing friends knowing the difficulties of trying to set up home during these arduous times.

Painting and papering, with the help of Chris and Pa, took my mind back to those early days when Kate and I splashed about in buckets of white-wash and paste; getting much more on ourselves than the job. We were little terrors. Smiling to myself, as I lifted a large brushful of paste, near to where Chris was trimming wall-paper, I suddenly laughed, while holding the brush at the ready. Chris eyed me, then the poised paste-brush and giggled, "Don't you dare! We've got to get this ruddy job finished, mi lad!"

"God! I'd luv t'give you a mustache," I chortled.

"Oh, would you, now. You'll be head first in that bucket, in a trice. Just hoppit, Chris guffawed.

"What's he up to now?" shouted mi dad, from the window.

"He wants t'paste my face, instead of the paper," tittered Chris.

"That's what he and young Kate used t'do. There was never a dull moment, I can tell you," laughed Pa. "Just nail 'is ruddy boots to the floor, Chris, with him in 'em!" We all collapsed laughing and I nearly kicked the paste bucket into the old fire grate.

With new lino on the bedroom floor and a sale price carpet square, the old place was beginning to take shape. A week or two later, Chris and I managed to buy a small, brand new bedroom suite at a Lewis's sale. We could hardly wait to see it arrive and set up in the recently-decorated bedroom. It was the first brand new thing either of us had ever had - apart from clothes and even some of those were second-hand. We worried about the money we'd spent but - well, what the hell - we were starting out in a new life together and we'd worked hard for this day.

Lewis's van arrived - in all its glory - and, nervously, we watched as the driver and his mate let down the tail-board and manhandled our bit of dream furniture out and up the stairs.

"Sign 'ere, will y'mam" the man said gruffly. Chris's hand trembled slightly as she signed the chit. Setting up the bed, positioning the dressing table and tiny chest of drawers was relativly easy as they weren't very heavy. It wasn't the stuff one would find in a mansion, but it was new - it was ours - it was part of a new home and a new life together. More things were needed but, for now, we just stood looking at our room - our little bedroom suite and then I glanced at Chris. Tears filled our eyes as I moved nearer and clasped Chris closely to me, kissing her gently on the cheek. "It's all ours, kid," I murmured, "and it's only the beginning. Someday, we'll make the 'Big Time' - we'll 'ave a big 'ouse - and a car and - and lots of cash," I cried convincingly.

Chris smiled and squeezed me, "There you go again, you and your pipe dreams! D'you reckon we could win the Pools, Bernie?" she questioned, hopefully.

"We might. No, not really, I'll just 'ave t'work that much 'arder and save until we bust. Then we might get a house on a mortgage." I replied.

"It'll be great 'ere with your mum and dad, but d'you really think we'll get a place of our own, later on, Bernie? I mean, it'd be very hard, wouldn't it?" Chris sighed.

"Why not? Ma and Pa did and they 'ad little enough, God knows."

"What's this about ma and pa?" Mum called as they both came upstairs to see the suite.

"Oh, Chris asked if we'd get a house, someday. I said that you had; why not we two."

"Of course you will," said Ma, emphatically, "things'll be better after the war and you're both good workers. As Bernie says, if we could, you can, luv."

"Yes," Pa chipped in, "you'll both make the grade eventually, kids. In the meantime, you're very welcome here - y'know that - and it's going to look great in these two rooms, when everything else is sorted out. I must remember to bring down that little clock for the mantel shelf. It brings the room to life a clock."

During the next few weeks, before the wedding, we collected innumerable pieces of furniture, ornaments and anything which served to turn our two small rooms into a very pleasant home within a home. After the honeymoon, even without our own house, we'd be able to share a happy life together. Excitement and enthusiasm for our very simple achievements might seem strange to some but, to us, who'd had little or nothing all our lives, every tiny step towards success and a better life, meant absolutely everything.

A rather strange thing happened when Ma, Chris and I were sorting out cupboards and rearranging furniture in the old dining room, our living room to be. From one cupboard there emerged a large, very old photo album. Idly glancing through the pages of faded sepia prints, I smiled at many old costumes and curious by-gone styles. Suddenly, I stopped - staring intently at a large, very pale portrait of an old gentleman with sideburns. A curious shiver ran the length of my spine.

"Ma," I questioned, "who's this old chap in the photo?"

Ma came across, put on her glasses, and peered at the album picture, "Why, that's your great grandfather, didn't you know? Haven't y'seen him before?" she asked.

"I well, no, that is, no, no, not really! I just wondered; he seems familiar, that's all." I mused.

"You've probably seen his picture at Gran's." Ma said, with little concern.

"Yes, you're right, I may have done." I murmured in agreement, but I suspected, nay, knew, as I looked again at the photo, that the old gentleman, smiling up at me from this faded print, was the very same one whom I'd seen on the little ferry boat, a few years ago. My thoughts drifted back to that lovely day on the Mersey ferry when our little 'Shirley Temple' girl had so amused us with her antics and I'd first asked Chris to marry me! The old man sitting opposite had nodded his approval and seemed to wish us well. I didn't know it then but I do now - it had been my great grandfather of that I'm absolutely sure! As I gazed, once again, at the kindly face in the pale photograph, I swear that I could feel his comforting presence there beside me now, wishing us both, God speed.

Chris leaned over to break the spell, "Is that your grandpa, then?" she asked, moving the album closer to the light."My great grand-father." I corrected.

"He looks a nice, kind, intelligent sort of chap, doesn't he? " Chris commented.

"Yes, yes, he does indeed, I wish I'd known him." I murmured.

"Known him," exclaimed Chris," he died long before you were born, for heaven's sake."

"Yes, of course, I know. Still, I'd like to know a bit more about him, someday." I whispered.

"You are a funny, sentimental old thing at times, aren't you?" Chris laughed.

"I guess so. Lord, we'd better get this damn job finished, hadn't we, darling?" I said.

"You're telling me,"Chris answered "Just save all those little daydreams of yours for later on."

Our spare time work soon completed the two rooms to our mutual satisfaction and, with a bit less stress, I went to make the necessary arrangements for a registry office wedding. Chris's mum and her brother (Chris's father being dead) organised the reception at a local hall in Smithdown Road. Ma had completed the wedding dress and two bridesmaids' dresses, having been away to check Kate's. Kate would be down for two days to attend the wedding. Ma was now in the business of putting finishing touches to both other garments, with Chris and young June on hand for fitting.

While Chris's mum and mine hovered around like mother hens, discussing and making final preparations, in an atmosphere of organised chaos, Pa and I kept well out of the way. It seemed safer that way. Well in advance of all this hustle and bustle, Chris and I had made enquiries at a couple of holiday spots, in Llandudno, recommended by friends. With little money to spare, we had to try for somewhere we could afford for our honeymoon. As luck would have it, the place we chose and were able to book, turned out to be so very nice that we returned many times after we'd married. Not all holiday residences, we heard later, were quite so pleasant as ours, particularly for nervous unsuspecting honeymooners.

However, with the honeymoon still a little way off, Chris and I, several weeks ahead of the Big Day, went on a ring hunting expedition. This was an occasion when we both wished that we had won the Pools. I joked that she might have to wear a curtain ring. After I'd rubbed my poor shins and apologised we trundled on. Settling, eventually, for a very nice but modestly priced ring, Chris turned to me, outside the jewellers, and whispered, "It's not just the ring, darling, but what you say and mean when you put it on," She smiled, doe eyed, and gently kissed my cheek.

"You'll know I mean every word, Chris, luv." Pausing, I murmured, "I do luv you, sweetheart with all my heart."

Her eyes moistened, "I know, luv, I know," she said, quietly and we kissed warmly, there in the street, despite the passers by.

Chris was well aware that most men, the night before they took the final plunge into matrimony, usually enjoyed an all male party with a few mates. As she so eloquently put it, " They hold a rowdy stag party, get tight and tell very rude jokes." She was probably right but, then again, perhaps girls do something similar. To me, getting 'tight-as-a-drum' just before the wedding, didn't seem a very good idea and, of course, Pa and I weren't really drinkers. Nevertheless, as Pa knew the landlord of the local hostelry, I did have a stag night at which a modicum of privacy had been arranged. Despite the privacy - or perhaps because of it a few friends got decidedly 'tipsy,' if not quite as newts. Expected good natured - though sometimes ribald remarks concerning my bachelor state and future loss of freedom emerged during the evening's revelry and caused a great deal of amusement at my expense. That poor, long suffering and much maligned creature, the mother-in-law featured in many unrepeatable stories, as did some of my previous mythical girl friends. In spite of the alcohol consumed, everyone carefully avoided naughty remarks about the bride-to -be. They all knew and loved Chris but wickedly wondered how she'd 'stuck me' so long.

In a slightly tipsy speech, near to the end of the proceedings, the Best Man laughingly apologised for any 'wisecracks' made during the evening and expressed his own and the company's good wishes and hopes for future happiness of the Bride and Groom ending with the words "And I know you all agree that Chris is a great gel and Bernie isn't a bad old stick either!" Shouts of 'Ear, ear' and 'Yes, they're a rollicking pair' or possible words to that effect.

While appreciating the sentiments expressed, I sincerely hoped that the Best Man would be a shade less inebriated by the following morning. Up jumped John, "Just one bit of advice, before we go Bernie, make the very best of the honeymoon because it's the last holiday you'll get before taking on a new boss!" Roars of very tipsy laughter! Of innumerable unrepeatable stories told, a rather silly one still lingers. It concerns the man arriving at a pub leading a snake on a bit of string. "Is that damn snake poisonous?" asked the landlord, in alarm. "Yes," said the man, unconcernedly. "Well, suppose it ruddy bites somebody, what d'you do?" exclaimed the landlord. "Just get a friend to suck out the poison," replied the man, coolly. Sarcastically, the landlord asked, "What if it 'shimmies' up my pants and bites my bum?" The man smiled, "Then you'll really find out who your friends are, won't you!"

Eventually, all going our separate ways, we drifted off on 'cloud nine' and I can vaguely remember Pa and me dreaming of an unreal tomorrow and hoping to God that we'd be in a reasonably stable condition in the morning.

Perfectly planned, the Big Day arrived. Nothing had been overlooked and yet I suffered from wedding morning nerves. Living together as man and wife would be a real test. Everyone, I told myself, has these doubts and fears but, whatever happened, I felt determined not to let Chris down; I loved her too much! Poor Chris, at her home with her admiring 'entourage' of helpers, the two mums and bridesmaids, must, I was sure, be feeling similar attacks of 'jitters.' My usual morning routine developed into feverish activity and, although the wedding wasn't until 2.30pm, I constantly checked the time.

With grey suit and tie neatly placed on the bed, I fished out socks, hankerchiefs and whatnot from the drawers just as George, Best Man, made his appearance. I must have asked George at least three times if he had the ring safe, before he managed to calm me down with a cup of coffee and the amusingly sarcastic remark that he, as Best Man, could take over if I was indisposed.

"You know," George said, highly amused, "in olden days, if the groom didn't turn up, the best man had to marry the bride in waiting."

"Oh, did he," I replied, equally amused "Well, you can forget that right now - I'll cut your ruddy feet off, for starters." Our feeble laughter, at a very mediocre joke, eased my nervous tension somewhat and we Pa, George and I finished dressing, complete with pink carnation button holes, and were ready to make the short journey to Wavertree Registry Office at about 1.30pm.

Sitting in the plain but warm ante-room, my worrying thoughts - the possible late arrival of the bride - were suddenly broken by a cheerful greeting from a photographer friend, armed with Nikon camera and tripod who'd promised to record the great occasion on hard to obtain film. Slowly drifting in, other friends and relatives greeted me but, somehow, I hardly seemed to hear.

With pounding heart and dry mouth, I nervously watched the door with increasing anticipation. Suddenly, she appeared - *My Chris*! Bridesmaids and others I hardly noticed for Christine, in her perfect wedding attire, looked lovelier and more attractive than ever before. She was absolutely radiant! In the bright electric light, Chris's eyes sparkled from beneath the flimsy white head-dress and veil she was wearing. The small bouquet she carried barely concealed the figure hugging bodice of her exquisite dress. To me, at that moment in time, Chris was so very beautiful, a vision of loveliness I'd never forget.

Quietly beckoned by the Registrar, I signalled to Chris who, taking her uncle's arm, smiled and followed me and the Best Man into the marriage room. Moments later, Chris was by my side. Gently squeezing her hand, I noticed the flush to her cheeks and the nervous smile flickering about her pretty lips. After routine questions and payment of the marriage fee, we were joined by our guests and the Superintendent Registrar who conducted the proceedings. As is customary, the Best Man placed the ring onto a small velvet cushion on the desk in front of us. Remembering Chris's early remarks outside the jewellers, we exchanged secret glances as the tiny gold symbol glinted in the light and the Registrar commenced the wedding ceremony.

With our vows clearly and strongly made, Chris lifted her veil and it was time for me to take the ring, proffered by the Best Man, to complete the marriage ceremony. The little gold band, which meant so much to both of us, slipped easily onto the outstretched finger of Chris's small, trembling hand. Clear blue eyes moistened as I embraced her and gently kissed her warm lips." I'll always luv you, darling" I whispered, very quietly.

Being now pronounced man and wife together, we had to sign the register and were followed by our two witnesses. The Registrar and Superintendent Registrar completed the entry with their signatures, and we were now truly married, at last. The rather sedate atmosphere soon turned to one of organised chaos as my photographer friend dodged about in a valiant effort to obtain good shots of the great event, including the register signing. As confetti throwing wasn't allowed inside the Registry, this boistrous activity would be recorded on the steps outside. Excitedly clutching the marriage certificate in her left hand, Chris held it aloft for all to see, to the cheers of, 'Good Luck,' 'A long and happy life,' and 'Best wishes for the future.' I turned, slipped my arm around Chris's waist and kissed my wife again. "Come on," I whispered, squeezing her. "Come on

TRUE LOVE: PHONEY CAKE! SUPPRESSING GIGGLES BEFORE CAMERA SHOT. -WEDDING-MAY-1944.
V.L.EDWARDS
PHOTO. POSING:-PRETENDING TO CUT 'FAKE CAKE!'

Mrs. Edmonds, it's time to go!" Chris giggled, her pretty face flushed with happiness." All right, Mr Edmonds, Dear Husband, let's go," she smiled as we left the Registry to pose on the steps, with everyone else, for the final photos, including the very boisterous confetti throwing caper.

Despite food rationing, the small reception was a great success, except for the fact that the large, three tiered wedding cake was a well crafted fake of icing sugar and cardboard. Complete with bells, bride and groom on the top tier and innumerable decorations, it certainly looked like the real thing. Nevertheless, a small, real, appetizing cake was concealed beneath the bottom tier. So, perhaps, we weren't really diddled. As Chris's father was dead, her Uncle Tom - knowing all of us well - delivered a short speech expressing his own sentiments and also those he believed Chris's dad would have wished on such a happy and memorable, family occasion.

In it, not only did he wish us happiness in our married life together but also mentioned that, over the years, my attitude towards Chris's mum had been that of a son. It was, as he put it, obvious that Chris and I were really meant for each other. After several amusing anecdotes, Uncle Tom concluded with a few words which stay in my mind. He said, " Make up your minds to be happy, the two of you, and you will be happy. Ladies and gentlemen, will you please rise and drink a toast to the Bride and Groom, Chris and Bernie."

Everyone cheered, stood up for the toast and then cried, "Speech, Speech." Very curious, no doubt, as to what I might say in this, my very first speech. Thanking everyone for attending the wedding and now the reception, I then said, "My wife and I." This caused uproar, cheers, table tapping and even a couple of wolf whistles. After the laughter had died down, I continued, with a broad grin, "Despite that uncalled for interruption," More quiet titters. "My dear wife and I are delighted to have you all here enjoying yourselves with us at this, the happiest time of our lives." Cheers and more low whistles. As silence again descended, I went on to thank my parents for their help and understanding and also Chris's mother and uncle for arranging a delightful reception for all of us. With grateful thanks from Chris and me to all who'd given us lovely presents, I concluded my short speech by paying tribute to our delightful bridesmaids, who'd contributed so much to this wonderful day and also, last but not least, to my Best Man whose invaluable help I greatly appreciated.

Looking across at the bridesmaids, I said, in a strong voice, "It is my honour and privilege now, ladies and gentlemen, to propose a toast to our beautiful bridesmaids who, Chris wishes me to say, have been so kind and helpful to her throughout all of the time up to and including the Wedding." I raised my glass, amidst tumultuous response." Ladies and Gentlemen, the Bridesmaids."

Guests obviously admired the bridesmaids and were well pleased with my first speech (Despite 'spotlight' nerves.)

Chris congratulated me on my effort, as did those close by. For several minutes, the room was filled with sounds of movement, laughter and general conversation before the Best Man rose to make his speech. Briefly mentioning the length of time he'd known Chris and me and the fact that I had been his responsibility until the actual wedding, he brought in the 'gag' concerning his duty to marry the bride if I failed to appear. This brought forth much hearty laughter and a round of applause. "Now," he continued, "with the beautiful bride married, I have the delightful duty of looking after our pretty bridesmaids. You'll all agree, I know, that the Bride and Groom make a wonderful couple and we wish them the best in health, wealth and happiness. This is a great day for them; it is their day alone: a day, I hope, they will always remember and treasure. Ladies and gentlemen, I now ask you all to rise and drink, with me, the toast of the Bride and Groom."

Response to the short, pleasant speech was immediate applause, clinking glasses and warm hearted cries of "To the Bride and Groom, long life and happiness." And out came the old hoary chestnut, "May all their troubles be little ones." One or two more photographs were taken before Chris and I managed to slip away for a quick change, closely followed by Ma and good old George who collected together our discarded apparel for return to the, now depleted, home wardrobe.

Uncle Tom kindly took our well packed holiday luggage to the front entrance, ready for a quick departure to Wavertree railway station. We had a first class compartment booked on the 5.30pm train bound for dear old Llandudno.

Leaving the reception - which obviously carried on after we left - was more of an ordeal than the Wedding, considering the amount of confetti, rice and comical remarks uttered by a few of the more tipsy guests. Arriving a bit early for the train we each, in turn, slipped into the station toilet to rid ourselves of extremely tenacious confetti. With a broad smile, Chris emerged onto the station platform and joked, "Y'know, there ought to be a law against this confetti lark, damn stuff gets everywhere."

"You're telling me, sweetheart," I grinned, giving Chris a quick 'peck' on the cheek as we both hurried forward with our luggage just as the old steam train, very slowly, whistled and puffed its way alongside our platform. I loved the old trains; still do - they were part and parcel of any holiday, at any time. I'm a kid still; just never grown up, I guess.

Being late arrivals, we'd missed the evening meal at our chosen guest house but Mrs. Thomas - bless her heart - after showing us our pleasant room, kindly prepared a snack - although we weren't really very hungry. She alone knew the secret of our first holiday together. "I do hope you'll 'ave a really nice stay, mi-dears," she said and then, with a twinkle in her eye, she whispered, "and a very, very happy life together, duckies. Best o'luck." She really was and still is, a kind and thoughtful person, one of the best.

Six other guests were taking advantage of the mild, Spring Llandudno air and so Chris and I were left alone in the cosy lounge, to relax and ponder on the past events of our very hectic day. The conversation covered everything from Chris's and the bridesmaids' early morning call and dressing, through the actual Wedding ceremony, the reception speeches and our final dash for freedom. Relaxed, we both yawned and laughed about the tense and amusing moments which had helped to make our day.

"Don't y'think we should go and unpack, darling?" I said, suddenly, "I want a wash, too, before the other guests get back."

"Yes, you're dead right, but," laughed Chris, "don't hog' the bathroom, I'll need it, too, y'know."

Upstairs we trekked to a very wide landing with doors on either side. Opening 'our' door, in front of Chris, I suddenly turned, grabbed her in my arms and lifted her bodily before she realised just what was happening.

"What the heck are y'doin,' put me down."

I smothered her giggling lips with mine before she said another word. "I'm carrying you over the threshold, you little minx!" I chortled, and kissed her again. By this time, I'd whisked her into the room, kicked the door shut and then, nearly falling over laughing, lowered Chris gently to her feet.

"You are a fool," Chris giggled, "but a very romantic one. Suppose somebody saw us."

"There's nobody on the landing - anyway, I don't care - do you?" I panted. Chris flung her arms round my neck and, crushing her lovely young body close to mine, we enjoyed lingering kisses.

"Oh, Chris, Chris, I do luv you," I whispered, ardently.

"Bernie. dearest, I've longed for this day," Chris murmured, her bright eyes shining, filled with deep emotion.

For those few precious moments, in a world of our own, we just clung together, without a word. Only sounds of other guests entering the house brought us down, with a bump, from 'cloud nine.'

"Bernie, luv," Chris sighed, "We'd better get our stuff sorted out, hadn't we? There's a nice wardrobe and plenty of drawer space. D'you think we've brought enough for a fortnight, Bernie?"

"Everything but the kitchen sink, I'd say." I laughed.

"You would say that; you men would go away with a tooth brush and just what you stood up in," Chris mockingly tittered.

Chasing her across the room to the suitcases, I playfully smacked her bottom. "Oh, would we, now," I chuckled.

"Eh, steady on." Chris chided, unlatching the first case, "Less slap and tickle, come on, now, let's empty these things and get the creases out." With great dexterity, Chris smoothed out the clothes and we tidied everything away.

"I'm off for a wash now, Chris, luv." I said, cheerily.

"O.K, but don't be long; the world and 'is wife'll want to get in that bathroom, shortly."

"Yeah, well, Pet, you be ready for a quick 'take over,' when I come out." I grinned.

With more than the soap and flannel on my mind, I tried to hurry and eventually dashed back to our room in my dressing gown. Chris, resembling a startled hare, shot out wearing her pink silk dressing gown and, armed with a very large sponge bag, hurried to the bathroom determined to seize the territory before someone else beat her to it.

Carelessly throwing off my dressing gown, I slipped between the cool, inviting sheets of the large double bed and nestled my head in one of its soft, frilly pillows. In a way, I relaxed yet my mind raced and my heart thumped. Constantly glancing towards the door, as the minutes passed, I breathed deeply to calm my senses. When Chris suddenly appeared, with her ravishing smile and flushed cheeks, my heart just literally missed a beat.

"Have I been very long?" she murmured, coyly. "I just want to fix my hair, darling."

She sat by the dressing table, with infuriating calmness, to finish her toilette. My pulse raced as I watched her in the mirror, putting on the slightest trace of makeup and a hint of scent, which drifted across the room towards me. God, I was on fire. She'd no idea how I felt. Beneath the sheets, I was hard and blood coursed hotly through my veins. Chris caught my gaze in the mirror and, smiling, she pursed her lips in a loving kiss.

"Darling," I croaked; my voice sounding very strange and dry, "Chris, sweetheart, come t' me, now," I pleaded, urgently.

Chris stood up, letting the dressing gown fall to the floor as she did so. Frilly black and pink silk panties just covered her upper thighs and hips and, as she kicked off slippers and turned towards me, my passionate gaze fell upon her ample bosom, flimsily concealed by a tightly fitting silky, pink bra.

Face and shoulders blushing crimson, Chris glided swiftly towards the bed with outstretched arms. I threw back the sheets, seized her hands and pulled her quickly to me. In an instant, her lovely breasts were crushed to my bare chest, as my eager arms encircled her near naked, trembling body. Inflaming desire, Chris's warm breath touched my cheek and quickly my ardent lips found hers. Suddenly, in the ardour of that passionate kiss, I felt her come alive as I slipped the bra from her shoulders and frantically, caressed her back. My nervous hands drifted down to remove the last vestige of silken clothing from her shapely thighs.

Quickly turning, with growing passion flooding through her loins, Chris frantically freed her legs of that final silken garment. Lying back, panting with desire, Chris seized my arms and pulled me ever closer to her quivering body. " Bernie, take me, now," she pleaded, urgently. "Oh, God, I need you, darling, take me." Caressing her arms, my fingers found hers and, pressing her hands deeply into the soft pillow, I quickly leaned forward, my senses reeling, and suckingly kissed the turgid nipples of her heaving breasts. Lovely legs tightly clasped my thighs and, as exquisite rapture surged within us both, we made frenzied, passionate love. Chris's whole quivering body melted into mine as if we were an indivisible part of each other. The sheer ecstacy of those perfect moments together, was exquisite and unforgettable.

Long after the deep but transient passion had slipped away, we lay together in profound contentment. Still pressed to her breasts, feeling the exciting throb of Chris's heart, I hoped and prayed that her love for me would remain as firm and strong as the constant, steady beat of that young heart. Slowly lifting my head, I gently kissed Chris's full, warm, crimson lips. Opening her eyes, she smiled up at me in complete happiness, "I do luv you, Bernie," she whispered, "Darling, it was wonderful."

"Chris, luv," I said, softly, "Luving together could never be more beautiful, you were marvellous, my angel."

"Oh, Bernie, Bernie, d'you really mean it? Was it all you'd hoped for ?" Chris asked, eagerly.

"You know it was, sweetheart, it was perfect in every way, my dear wife."

Kissing her forehead and eye-lids, I once again, kissed her inviting lips as we clung together in a further ardent, naked embrace.

While gently moving apart and about to drift into a deep, tranquil and satisfying sleep, I realised - and I'm sure Chris did too - that we were so lucky to be physically suited, so lucky to have enjoyed a perfect, first experience. Wondrous tales of perfect honeymoon bliss didn't always materialise for many but, as I sleepily watched my beautiful, slumbering bride, I knew we were compatible. Without a doubt, we were ideal mates.

I need hardly say that we missed breakfast time by a 'mile.' Dear, understanding Mrs. Thomas - out of earshot of other guests - murmured, as she nudged Chris, "Believe it or not, dearie, I was a blushin' young bride, once. Cor, that weddin' an' reception. Lordy, that was a day an' an 'arf, I can tell ya." Chris, Mrs T. and I 'fell apart' laughing. "See, I was cockney," continued Mrs T, "an' John, gawd rest 'is soul, was Welsh. Yes, that was 'is name, John Thomas." We all guffawed again.

"Best if they'd slipped 'im a middle name, wouldn't it, dearie?" she laughed. "Unless, that is, they'd made it 'Willy." Again, we all chortled like three school kids.

Recovering, Mrs. Thomas went on, "Look, lav, never mind the comedy, would you like a bite of breakfast, na," she paused, grinning, "you an y'r husband?"

Chris giggled,"Oh, would it be a lot of bother? We're awful late."

"No bother at all, lav," said Mrs T. and then added with a wink, as she toddled down the hall, "Long as y'don't make an' abit of it, dearie."

"She's really great, isn't she?" I chuckled, as Chris and I strolled, dreamily, into the pleasant dining room to await our very late breakfast.

Sunny, fairly mild May weather enabled us to get out and about every day during that first glorious week of our honeymoon. Becoming friendly with John and Madge, the youngest of three other couples staying here, we were just leaving the house - about the the second morning - when John patted my back and said, "Another great day, old man, hope you both enjoy it," and then, with a curious smile, he flicked the lapel of my coat with his finger, "Just a bit of cotton or something, that's better; it showed up on the blue cloth, y'know. Anyway, see you later, have a nice time" Madge waved goodbye and we thought no more about it.

Returning, that same evening, we were chatting to John and Madge, in the lounge, about the day, when John said, "Yes, we were watching the kids building sand castles on the beach, - they were having a whale of a time."

"By jove, yes,"Madge cut in, "I love t'see the children happy, don't you, Chris?"

"Oh, aye, it makes my day." answered Chris. And then, before Chris could comment further, Madge, with a strange smile, looked straight at Chris and said, "Have you got any kids, Chris?"

Poor Chris blushed to the roots of her hair and stammered, "Er, no, no, not yet."

"Have you been married long?" John questioned, glancing at Madge.

"Well, no, no, not long, not very long." Chris replied, looking rather embarrassed.

Madge couldn't keep a straight face and chortled, "It's a shame to pull their legs, John."

"You mean.." I started to say.

"Yeah," smirked John, "that bit of cotton on your coat, this morning, was confetti, old boy. And, well, we put two and two together and guessed, Bernie."

Chris, still blushing, laughed out loud and playfully slapped Madge's arm, "What do you mean, 'have I got any kids, you've got a nerve." They both laughed heartily and Madge came over and kissed Chris. "Don't I get one?" I cried, with feigned disappointment.

"But, of course," Madge tripped across and kissed my cheek.

"This calls for a small celebration," John exclaimed,"It's our second wedding anniversary next week, so why don't we all have a meal at that little place top of Mostyn Street. What y'say?"

"Oh, great, that'd be luvly, wouldn't it,Bernie?" enthused Chris.

"Sure would!" I replied, "D'you know, John, I'm not surprised you spotted that confetti, this morning, I shifted the damn stuff from behind both lapels and I'll bet my top pocket's full of it."

"Never mind," tittered Chris, "leave it there; it'll remind you of the day we got married."

Now with the 'cat out of the bag,' so to speak and much conversation about the Wedding and our home town, we were really delighted to discover that our new found friends hailed from Birkenhead. The lasting friendship formed with John and Madge, at that time, had a particular significance for us in future years, since we'd met them while on our memorable honeymoon.

Although, with kind understanding, they left us to enjoy our special time alone together, we did,on several days, make a 'foursome' and their jovial company brought a real breath of fresh air to a wonderful holiday. A fortnight soon passes when one is in love but, at least, Chris and I had a lovely, if unpretentious, well decorated home to which we returned. Many, in these hard times, were not so fortunate. Our married life had started well in what, no doubt, numerous folks would have considered to be almost the 'lap of luxury.' Times do change.

My dear sister, Kate, along with young June, in their beautiful dresses, had both bid us an emotional farewell and wished us well on our departure to Llandudno. Now, in a long letter, just received from the hospital, it seemed that Kate was making steady progress and enjoying the work, but I could detect a longing for home. Thoughts of poor Kate's solitary - if busy and interesting life compared to our own rapturous happiness, tugged hard on my heart-strings. I loved Kate so very much. No man could wish for a better sister.

CHAPTER 6

Early trauma for Kate. Our Happy Event.

Back at home, Chris and I settled in nicely to our cosy 'nest', with the help of Ma and Pa, and returned to our wartime work. Kate was still fully occupied on emergency ward duties at the hospital. With a bit of luck, we hoped to be able to visit her before Christmas.

In the Emergency Ward, Kate was soon to learn, the hard way, one of the main principles of becoming a good State Registered Nurse. Private study and the acquisition of practical skills was vital, of course, but learning to handle one's emotions, in traumatic situations, isn't at all an easy task.

From the outset, students were instructed to be caring and considerate but were warned never to become emotionally involved with any patient. Obviously, undue emotion could seriously affect the smooth, efficient running of any hospital. At times, poor Kate found this 'pill' very hard to swallow.

Early one morning, the ambulance clanged up to the hospital entrance bringing in a young woman found to be covered in bruises and with a broken arm and suspected fractured rib. In a lot of pain, she was accompanied by a burly, sour faced individual, showing 'theatrical' concern for her welfare. Red eyed and reeking of alcohol, he stupidly complained that he'd 'ad a few' and was sorry that he'd 'knocked er about a bit' when she'd refused his attentions.

As the poor girl was whisked away for X-ray and treatment, closely followed by Kate, the resident officer, Dr Jones, directed a few well chosen, vitriolic remarks towards the husband, concerning wife beating, before turning to follow the patient's trolley.

'Boozy' human behaviour was nothing new. Many times, Kate had witnessed the effects of drink and the trouble it caused, but when it resulted in the hospitalisation of a slim, young girl in this way, Kate found it hard to remain objective and to hide her feelings.

Not so very long after this minor incident - comparatively minor for E.W - a serious accident case was rushed in from the ambulance. As the Sister in charge and young Doctor Jones swiftly moved forward to make an initial examination, Kate, waiting to one side for instructions, could see a small figure, covered by a blanket, lying on the trolley. Pillow and blanket were, ominously, stained with blood.

Quickly taken to a side room, adjoining the operating theatre, the unconscious patient was carefully lifted onto a small white bed. Under Sister's instructions and with her help, Kate nervously proceeded to clean up and prepare the unfortunate victim - a young girl in her mid-teens. Beneath the dirt and blood they carefully removed, Kate, trembling very slightly, could see blood trickling from a ghastly wound in the forehead. Sister's expression was one of deep concern.

As Doctor Jones set up a plasma drip, prior to a possible transfusion, and Sister quickly sought the uneven, frighteningly rapid pulse in the girl's wrist, she murmured, almost inaudibly, "She's bleeding, deepening unconsciousness. Intra cranial haemorrhage."

Awaiting the surgeon, Kate found herself desperately trying to fight her emotions. The girl was so pretty, so young and with all her life before her, but that life was rapidly draining away.

Mr Nixon, the surgeon, appeared, "X-rays, yet?" he questioned, curtly.

"No, Sir, radiologist is here now with the portable." Sister answered.

"Be quick, man - no time to lose," Mr Nixon barked at the Radiologist.

X-ray pictures quickly taken and removed for processing, the surgeon immediately turned to the patient. Carefully checking the wound, pulse and blood pressure, he finally listened to the chest.

"Get her to theatre, Sister, do mi best to remove those bone splinters - hardly need an X-ray - but chances are a bit slim. How the devil did it happen?" Mr Nixon asked.

"Policeman's notes indicate she'd been forcibly thrown from a bike and into a stone wall, when struck by a speeding car which failed to stop," Dr. Jones replied.

"Good God! Swine - I hope they catch the bastard! What sort of animal would do that? There must be plenty of other 'scum' in the world besides those Nazi thugs!" Mr Nixon exclaimed, with understandable anger. "If you can prepare theatre quickly, Sister, we'll do our best to save the poor kid," he added, showing obvious concern.

X-rays, soon available, were carefully studied by Mr. Nixon, prior to his unenviable task.

In the operating theatre, Kate, as junior nurse, stood by ready to tie on the doctor's gowns and perform any other duties required, while Sister prepared the patient for surgery. With dry mouth and thumping heart, Kate prepared to witness her first operation. Small it would be, no doubt, but careful, delicate skill would be required to remove fragments of bone from soft brain tissue.

When the time came, Kate watched with strange fascination as the surgeon, a hefty man, with unbelievable dexterity and perfect concentration, performed his delicate task. An anaesthetist constantly checked his equipment, while Dr. Jones and Sister Brady were on hand at either side of the operating table.

Suddenly, something seemed terribly wrong, excessive spurts of vivid, red blood. Feverish activity to find and quell the arterial flow, and then the girl stopped breathing. Desperately, the two doctors tried to restart the heart. Hesitating only for a moment, surgeon Nixon, directing a piercing glance at Sister Brady, pointed quickly to the tray of instruments, "Direct heart massage," he almost shouted. Sister thrust the required knife into Dr. Jones' hand and, before Kate could fully comprehend the situation, the now lifeless girl's chest was swiftly and deftly opened for direct heart massage.

Averting her gaze from the sudden, unexpected scene and the surgeon's bloody, probing fingers, Kate trembled from head to foot; she felt cold and desperately fought to keep control of her confused mind and quivering body. Uncontrollably, she swayed and then just managed to grab a chair back and slide quietly onto the seat, trying, as she did so, to regain a clear head.

The medical team didn't even notice as they fought to save the patient's life. Pumping the respiration bag, the anaesthetist desperately tried to fill the lungs with oxygen, through an inserted tracheal tube, as the heart massage proceeded. Stimulant injected directly into the heart muscle proved ineffective and blood pulsation slowly disappeared. It was too late; the heart stopped. The young girl was dead.

Still seated, pale and trembling slightly, Kate breathed deeply, determined to regain her all important composure. Ceasing their frantic efforts, the two doctors looked at each other and then pulled down their face masks. They'd done everything possible.

Drawing the sheet up to completely cover the dead girl, Mr Nixon, for the first time, noticed Kate's sad, white face. Looking steadily at Sister Brady, he said, " Sorry Sister, you know the score, it was probably inevitable." Then, as Kate glanced towards him, he said, quietly, "I'm afraid, nurse, we don't always win. Casualty can be a hard school. Emergency surgery and the trauma involved can be very disturbing. In time, my dear, you'll learn to cope."

Although very flattered that a man of Mr. Nixon's standing should even bother to consider the feelings of a junior nurse, Kate was deeply annoyed with herself for having succumbed to a stupid, yet predictable reaction. Standing up, head high, although her legs still trembled, Kate said clearly, in a firm voice, "Sir, Sister, I must apologise for my temporary loss of personal control, in theatre. It won't happen again Sister."

Somewhat taken aback by these remarks, Mr. Nixon glanced shrewdly, with the flicker of a smile, at Sister Brady and then, after a moment Sister said quietly, "On the contrary, Nurse Edmonds, your demeanour during a first encounter with radical surgery and the subsequent death of a patient has been admirable. I've noted your work and progress, Kate, and you possess the qualities required by a good nurse."

Mr Nixon, slowly removing his surgical gloves, nodded approval. "Yes, indeed." he murmured as he slipped off his gown, preparing to leave the theatre. Dr. Jones smiled at Kate. Blushing slightly, Kate replied, "Thank you. Sister. Sir, I'll do my best. Shall I return to the ward?"

"Er, no, assist me here, for the moment, and don't carry on with your normal duties, nurse" Sister seemed, Kate thought, to emphasise the word Nurse.

As Kate later left the theatre, she carried with her, in her mind's eye, the approving glance of Sister Brady. Suddenly, she felt so proud of her simple status as a student nurse. During the many weeks that followed, Kate sometimes thought of Mr. Nixon's words as she rapidly became - not hard - but conditioned to the numerous, difficult situations and very frequent traumas which continually faced her, and the rest of the hospital staff. Kate was not only growing up very quickly as a person, she was developing and growing up as a nurse, she was becoming a professional.

Having already had preliminary training, Kate was now under contract with the hospital authorities for a full training period of four years.

We, at home, soon noticed the change in Kate's outlook, on the odd occasions when we were able to see her. She was still our Kate but she had become so adult, so worldly and shrewd. Our young Kate had grown up fast, without a doubt.

In these rapidly changing times and the sort of world she'd encounter, Kate's strong will and steadily maturing attitude were assets she'd really need to make her way in the nursing profession.

A few weeks before Christmas '44, Chris, complaining of tummy upset, had been to see the doctor. One evening, as we both settled down on the small settee, in front of a nice, warm coal fire in our cosy sitting room, Chris told me that she'd been to see the GP again.

"What did he say?" I asked, casually, from behind my newspaper.

"Oh, well, y'see, last week, I took a sample." Chris answered, nervously.

"A sample?" I questioned, putting down the paper.

"Yeah, y'know 'wee' in a bottle. And well, he said - he said he thought I might - I was pregnant."

"Pregnant," I echoed; more in surprise than anything, really.

Suddenly sitting back, poor Chris, her eyes wide with concern, said apologetically, "Gosh, Bernie, I'm sorry, I know we didn't plan it so soon. Are you upset, luv?"

Quickly realising how my voice must have sounded, I smilingly grabbed her hand and pulled her close to me. "You daft 'apeth. Why should I be upset f'eaven's sake? I'm pleased; I know you've always wanted kids," laughingly, I squeezed her.

"I know, Bernie, but are y'really pleased. I mean, it'll be, well, another mouth t'feed, won't it?" Chris murmured, anxiously.

"Don't worry, we'll get by - we 'ave up to now. Anyway, I've always fancied 'aveing' - I was going to say a son - but it might be a little girl, mightn't it?" We both laughed, joyously.

"Would y'mind if it was a girl, I mean?" Chris asked, curiously.

"No, course not; I know you want a little girl. Don't deny it, I remember that day on the boat," I chuckled.

Chris looked a bit bemused, "On the boat?" she questioned.

"Yeah, you remember, when that little 'Shirley Temple,' with 'er bag of sweets, sat opposite us on the ferry boat. When I first asked you t'marry me. Come on," I prodded her in the ribs. "Don't 'cod on' you've forgotten, y' little minx."

Chris giggled and slapped me, "Gosh, yes, I remember. - Oh, God, she was luvly, wasn't she? I do hope our kid's like that." For a moment Chris was lost in her own happy memories.

"There you are," I kidded, bringing her back down to earth, "you do want your own little Shirley Temple." I put my arms round Chris and, holding her tightly, I kissed her warm lips.

"I do luv you, sweethearts," I whispered, "both of you."

Tears filled Chris's lovely eyes and, hugging me, she pressed her soft cheek to mine. We were both so very, very happy; we were both so very young.

"Look luv, have y'told your mum or my ma?" I asked, with some concern.

"Don't be daft, Bernie, I've only just found out, 'aven't I?" Chris tittered.

"Yes, course, I forgot." I smiled.

"There's only one thing worries me, Bernie," Chris said, fearfully, "d'you think this terrible war'll be over before she's born? I mean, it's been on for years now

"Oh God Bernie, I don't want the baby born into this 'stinkin' war," Chris trembled in my arms, a look of dismay in her eyes.

"Chris, luv, don't upset y'self , not now, the ruddy war'll be over next year, I know! They're knockin' hell out of the Germans everywhere. With the Yanks in now, they'll beat jerry into the ground," I exclaimed, doing my best to reassure her.

"God, I hope you're right, Bernie, I only hope you're right."

"Course I'm right, luv. You just think of having our baby; it'll be born in the Peace, you'll see. Come on kid, don't upset the 'ba-be.' Where's that big smile you've always had."

Chris grinned up at me, "You're a born optimist, aren't you, ducky." She kissed my cheek.

"It's a good job somebody is, round 'ere" I joked, "and I'll tell y'something else, darlin', all those so called pipe dreams of mine are comin' true as well - eventually." I hugged Chris tightly and kissed her.

"Hey, steady on, don't squeeze so flippin hard," she smirked and we both took a fit of the giggles.

1945 certainly was a better year and my forecast about the ghastly War was one prediction that did come true. On May 8th, Mr. Winston Churchill broadcast his historic V.E Day message to the Nation, officially confirming the 'cessation of hostilities' - the end of the War in Europe.

All gathered round the wireless at home. Our feelings, our thoughts were so very different from those we had on that terrible September day way back in 1939, when War had been declared.

New hopes for the future, reflected in everyone's eyes, gladdened my heart as I looked across the room at Chris's beaming smile. My Chris, now almost six months pregnant, looked radiantly happy. "What did I tell y'Chris," I shouted over, "The War's over kid, it's over and the baby isn't due 'til August. Now will you believe your 'old man'."

Chris, still with a broad smile, gave the 'thumbs up' and blew me a big kiss.

Still listening to the wireless, after the Prime Minister's broadcast, we heard the previous night's recorded commentaries and uproarious sounds from scenes, up and down the country of delirious crowds thronging the streets everywhere. Mad with delight, as news came in last night - 7th May - the people shouted,

"It may be V.E Day tomorrow, but the ruddy War's over tonight."

In London, thousands thronged the great thoroughfares - Piccadilly, The Mall and outside Buckingham Palace. Waving flags, shouting, singing, marching with linked arms, couples kissing and cuddling; everyone went mad. Cheering and shouting never ceased as the multitudes, drunk with happiness, pushed and jostled, laughingly waved flags and kissed anyone at hand. It was a scene of unbelievable pandemonium; delirious jubilations born of utter thankfulness and relief at the end of five long years of total War.

Liverpool, Birkenhead, Manchester and all the big cities were the same. Hope, at last, for some sort of future with joyous relief and happiness showing in people's faces. The atmosphere was electric and almost tangible; one could put out a hand and touch it, or so it seemed. Everyone hoped against hope that this euphoria would last and really lead to a better life; a better world.

Vexing obstacles would, however, still beset the lives of many, including us.

Chris and I couldn't afford to worry unduly about others' troubles I'm afraid, as we'd probably have enough of our own. Although more than glad that the war was over, I knew that life wasn't going to be easy. It never had been; it wasn't going to change overnight. We'd need to do a lot of hard work and, perhaps, have a bit of luck, before our lifestyle would alter very much. Nevertheless, I intended to have a damned good try to improve our lot, and I knew Chris was with me all the way on that score.

At the moment, Chris, bless her heart, was coping well with her strange, new physical condition. I soon learned, however, that bearing a child wasn't necessarily the simple, straightforward, natural phenoma that many - particularly men - would have us believe. Chris's 'morning sickness' subsided in about, I suppose, the first two or three months but, apart from the obvious inconvenience of increased size and weight, she was, as so often happens, plagued by minor, though uncomfortable, pregnancy complaints during the passing months.

Strange as it may sound, I felt peculiarly aware, at times, of Chris's inner feelings. Much as, I should imagine, someone might experience regarding their twin. Whether or not other men have noticed this strange emotion I really don't know. Perhaps, as Chris says, I've got too much imagination.

Hilda Smith, Ma's lifelong friend and experienced midwife, probably thought so too, but her friendly advice was always forthcoming throughout difficult days. She understood the stress encountered by couples during a first pregnancy.

Despite our desire for a child and the thrill of becoming parents, I knew we'd both be relieved when the pregnancy was over. A normal, healthy baby was the hope of every couple but, until the actual birth, nothing was really certain. Unknown to Chris, I constantly worried about the outcome and I'm sure she did too. Thinking of our forebears with their very large families, I couldn't help wondering how they managed to cope with multiple pregnancies. They deserved a medal.

Our Kate's helpful, reassuring letters were a very welcome encouragement to us both. Chris was delighted to know that Kate, her best friend since early childhood, really cared about her and our unborn baby's future welfare. Long and detailed; Kate's letters were better than any doctor's tonic, to Chris.

All of us longed for the day when Sister Kate would be home again for good. On completion of her training Kate might, we hoped, secure a suitable nursing situation here, in dear old Liverpool. Meantime, for her very thoughtful consideration, she always remained in our thoughts with deep affection

Now nearly mid-August in this glorious victory year of 1945 and very close to Chris's 'time,' I'd already discovered that pregnancy involved innumerable examinations and tests which dear Chris seemed to take in her stride. It was, I thought, a good thing that men don't have babies. The first would be the last, I'm sure. Joking apart, we couldn't complain about the help and support we'd received from everyone during the previous months. Since confirmation that Chris was having a baby, our family doctor, who'd treated us all from childhood, had agreed that Hilda Smith should be midwife to care for Chris in the period of her confinement.

Now, as everything appeared to be straightforward, the doctor decided that Chris could have her baby at home. We were delighted and Chris felt so much more at ease knowing that Hilda, whom she'd come to know and trust so well, would be there to deliver her child. Dr. Jones assured us too, that he would endeavour to be available, should the need arise.

Outwardly confident, poor Chris, in her quieter moments, was really a bit scared. As a girl, she'd heard so many 'old wives' tales of things that could happen and just hoped her fears were unfounded. Silently, I shared Chris's apprehension but Hilda's frequent, reassuring visits were a blessing to us both.

Just before seven in the morning, on August 20th, I dashed out to fetch the midwife. With typical inexperienced panic - convinced the baby was on its way - I almost ran the two blocks to Hilda's house. Gasping out the details to a sympathetic nurse, I lurched into the lobby and, panting hard, leaned against the wall.

"Calm down, Bernie, luv," Hilda exclaimed, "They don't pop out like a cork y'know, it takes time. Her contractions'll be a lot closer, lad, before she's due."

Mr. Smith appeared from the kitchen, "For heaven's sake, sit down, son!" he cried, looking at my trembling hands, "Good God lad, anybody'd think *you* were 'aveing the kid."

"I know, but d'you think she'll be alright?" I cut in anxiously, "Ma's with 'er but she's not a nurse," I added nervously.

"Don't worry, Bernie," Hilda reassured me, "We'll be there in ten minutes and, believe me, it'll take a lot longer than that."

A little calmer, I sat down. "You're the midwife, Hilda, I know you're right, it's just, well, I had to come and make sure, I'm not used to these things."

"You did the right thing Bernie. I know the first child's a big strain." Hilda leaned forward and patted my arm, "I've delivered a few, y'know luv, and the first usually likes to take his or her time to come into this funny old world of ours. Come on now Bernie, let's go, Chris'll be fine. In a few hours you'll both be proud, happy parents, a mum and dad."

Of course, experienced nurse Hilda was right about the time, and it was nearly noon before she informed me there'd been a 'show' and that labour could be starting. I didn't need telling twice to forward the midwife's comments to Dr. Jones via the 'phone at the top of our street.

Our family doctor's presence - soon after labour commenced - was a real confidence boost to me. Now, I thought, my dear Chris was in the capable hands of a full team, I was very lucky.

Nevertheless, I was 'on pins,' sitting down, standing up, nibbling biscuits and walking about for no apparent reason. Eventually, settling on an easy chair in our dining room, I must have dozed off through sheer lack of sleep. Sudden footsteps on the polished lino jolted me from an uneasy slumber. Ma walked into the room and, involuntarily, I stood up, half awake. "Is she, is she alright?" I croaked, trying to clear my throat.

Ma beamed, "She's fine - resting now - she's very tired but she's okay and so is your *Daughter*, Bernie"

"A Girl, oh, great," Chris really wanted a daughter. "And she's okay. Thank God."

I grabbed my ma and we both hugged one another and, I'm not ashamed to say, I sobbed like a kid. Slowing stifling my emotions, I said nervously, "Can I see them now, will it be alright, Ma?"

"Course y'can, Bern, but not like that, for God's sake." Ma giggled, "Wipe y'face, y' daft 'apeth."

"I'll 'ave a quick 'swill'" I sniggered, "and then go up there. Tell them I'm on my way to see my two best girl friends." With an elfish grin at Ma, I dashed off to the kitchen.

Daft as it sounds, my nerves were playing tricks as I reached the bedroom and I even knocked 'gingerly' on the door.

Hilda's voice called out, "Come in *Dad*."

There was Chris, against the pillows, smiling broadly and with the small covered bundle held close to her breast. "Bernie, luv, come and see our daughter," she called, triumphantly.

Nervously. I went over and peered at the so tiny scrap of living, breathing humanity. Quite oblivious of others in the room, I bent forward and kissed Chris."You've got your *own* little 'Shirley Temple' now, luv," I murmured. "She's luvly. I'm really 'appy, Chris, I luv y'both."

Chris smiled happily but looked so pale and exhausted. "Look, Chris, are you O.K, luv?" I asked, rather stupidly.

"I'll be fine in a day or two, Bernie," she whispered, shakily, "they've all been so good to me." Weeping a bit, she closed her eyes and her mum came over to lift the baby gently and put it into the warm crib.

It was only then that I really noticed others in the room. Tactfully, they'd all kept quiet until I'd seen the baby and talked to Chris. Sinking easily into the soft pillows, Chris seemed to murmur something and then drifted into a shallow sleep.

"I think we ought to let 'er rest awhile, Bernie," Hilda whispered, "she's still drowsy after the 'twilight sleep' drug. Sleep is a great healer luv. She looks so peaceful, now, doesn't she?"

Indeed she did, and lovely too. Desperately, I wanted to hug her tightly and whisper thanks for our new-born child but now, I knew, the gentle therapeutic slumber, to soothe her mind and body, was the thing she needed most.

I'd known Chris so long - since we were kids together - and, watching her sleeping form, I realised how lucky I was to have such a wife. No husband could wish for a better partner and now our baby would cement the loving bond between us.

Soon, we chose pleasant sounding Emily, after Chris's grandmother, as baby's first name. A second name - Shirley - sprang to mind from our happy memories of my proposal to Chris on board the Mersey Ferry boat. Mischievous little 'Shirley Temple' as we'd called her, had won our hearts, that day, as she'd scampered happily along the boat deck with her bag of sweets.

Beautiful baby Emily Shirley was the centre of our world. No other kid was, or could be, quite like her, or so we thought.

"You and that baby," laughed sister Kate; down on a visit, "Anyone'd think you were the first and only pair to have one." And then she'd cuddle and kiss the gurgling little mite even more than we did. She really loved our child.

As a nurse, Kate saw many babies during her working life but little Emily always occupied a special place in her heart. Considering we three musketeers' life-long bond, Kate's deep affection for our baby wasn't surprising.

Caring for baby and home was a full time job and so Chris left work with the promise of reinstatement later on if she needed employment.

Now with three mouths to feed, I not only worked overtime but, having studied modern technology, serviced and repaired wireless sets in my spare time. Although 405 line television restarted after the War on the 7th June 1946, a Victory Parade was televised the next day, 8th June, but we in Liverpool couldn't yet receive the transmissions. Broadcasting from Holme Moss didn't commence until 1951.

Rapidly developing still and cinematography were of great interest to both Chris and me but time and money, in the early days of our marriage, meant that such time-consuming, expensive hobbies needed to be shelved for a while.

Round about mid-1946, life became a little difficult for

us at home when Ma developed acute bronchitis. After a couple of weeks, her worsening condition and terrible 'puppy dog' cough, which kept us all awake at night, was very distressing. Medical attention helped, I suppose, but she lost weight and became weary through loss of sleep. Frightened for little Emily's health, with good reason, no doubt. Chris, feeling very guilty, kept baby well out of harm's way.

With Ma now in her mid fifties, unless something could be done quickly to check the illness, it could become chronic. Firstly, Dr. Jones got a number of chest X-rays taken and then started Ma on a further course of treatment. Progress appeared painfully slow and it was several months before she seemed to throw off the unpleasant infection. Although the cough and other symptoms disappeared, it took a long time for her to regain weight, energy and a real feeling of well being. Ilness was something that Ma and Pa weren't used to. As Ma once said, laughingly, 'We never ever had time to be ill.' They are pretty tough, the pair of them.

Despite the general upset of her grandma's illness, baby Emily's growth and development was very good - marvellous, to us. In less than twelve months her weight had tripled and noticeable increasing mental awareness was a constant source of amusement to everyone.

"Of course," I said, trying to keep a straight face,"Emily is bound to possess her father's intelligence and inherit his undoubted capabilities."

Highly amused, Chris laughingly cried, "Oh, will she, now. God forbid."

Pa had made the baby a play-pen and, even at nine months, she'd pull herself up the side and try to walk. Words like 'mama' and 'dada,' she'd try to say, were just about discernible and she'd play 'peekaboo' and wave bye-bye; although strangers made her shy - perhaps being a little girl.

Just after her first birthday, Emily walked, if held by one

hand and, of course, played with toys. Pa, always good with kids, laughed at her desire to put things on her head, chuck everything out of the pen and constantly lift toys and what-not in and out of boxes and buckets. Outside, Emily's attention was drawn to everything. With great interest, she gazed at animals and other children and seemed fascinated by motor cars! Perhaps she'd been a driver in a former life.

A long, bitterly cold wintry spell at the start of 1947 was an anxious time for Chris and me, baby's warmth and welfare. Snow outside our kitchen window seemed a very strange sight to tiny Emily - she wondered what on earth it was.

Constant, almost weekly, changes in baby behaviour, made it easy to answer Kate's many questions, in her letters, concerning her beloved niece's progress. At home, I'd sometimes catch Chris with that look, which only mothers have, watching, with affection, her offspring's antics as she played and grew steadily older by the minute. By Spring '47, when our little darling was about eighteen months old, she was walking really well, hardly ever fell over and Ma and Pa proudly watched her climb up into large easy chairs or slide easily into little ones. Watching adults watching her, Emily seemed to sense her own tiny achievements and tried hard to please and be noticed.

Chris, while knitting, often nudged me from my newspaper to watch our 'favourite' daughter pulling toys or, best of all, carrying her cherished doll whilst murmuring gibberish into its tiny ear. Copying adults and trying to talk - now with about ten or so words - was such a thrill to us, a thrill that only other parents can understand.

Unearthing some coloured picture books, Grandpa soon became Emily's favourite person as he patiently explained to her the simple stories. Gleefully pointing at a page, she'd name familiar things. Sometimes, sensing a mistake, she'd giggle and pout, coyly looking up at Grandpa. For a moment Emily would ponder, whilst sucking a tiny thumb and then a little podgy finger would suddenly prod the picture in triumph, as she cried out the right name. Grandpa's patience with these simple picture stories helped the little mite a great deal, in her early months of learning. He was a good teacher.

As 1947 drew to a close, another memorable royal event hit the headlines; the Wedding - on November 20 - of Princess Elizabeth and Prince Philip.

Many memories of glittering pageantry of the 1937 Coronation returned and great excitement swept the Nation as it was realized that one of the two beloved, real life princesses was to be married.

Although little Emily didn't fully understand the significance of the great event, she listened intently to the broadcast wireless commentary, with the rest of us, and, no doubt, thought that fairy tales do really come true. (Like her dad's pipe dreams).

She'd seen beautiful princesses in her picture books and, perhaps, visualized Princess Elizabeth - our future Queen-to-be - as one of those angelic creatures who had suddenly materialized from between the pages of her wonderful fairy-tale books.

Maybe she dreamed of being a princess, herself, one day and meeting her own handsome prince. Emily, pretty and wide eyed was, to Chris and me, already a beautiful little princess.

CHAPTER 7

Emily's first holiday, Kate's success.

With books and wireless - possibly records - being the only home entertainment or, maybe, aid to learning, Emily, like the rest of us, would have to wait about five years before a primitive black and white television would be available to help or amuse her. A children's T.V. programme had started as early as 7th July 1946 but as Holme Moss, the transmitter to cover Merseyside, was not yet built, Liverpool had to be content with wireless.

After a very hard winter, we decided to take Emily, now aged nearly two, for her first seaside summer holiday. Never having seen kids building sand castles or even glimpsing the seashore, except in picture books, she must have felt a bit bewildered and very excited about going away on the 'big puffer.' Now with a little boy, Simon, about Emily's age, our Birkenhead friends, John and Madge, had managed to book the same holiday period at Mrs Thomas's lovely guest house in Llandudno. Chris and I felt thrilled at the idea of holidaying once again with the couple we'd first met on our honeymoon.

Excellent 'digs' and a promising weather outlook were a very encouraging start for our August break and we all quickly settled in. Emily, although having seen Simon once before, was a bit shy at first but after we'd all 'trekked' down to the beach armed with buckets and spades - reticence began to fade, the 'ice' began to melt and both kids became good and very boisterous pals.

It's really marvellous to watch how the sight of sand and sea can actually 'get kids going.' I'll never forget the look on

Emily's face when first she saw noisy, blue water rolling up the beach. In bare feet and little frilly costume, she chased the receding wavelets and then, giggling gleefully, she ran like mad as they chased her back. A couple of times, she tripped back and forth and then stood back to watch 'macho' Simon stamping his feet in the foaming briny. With head cocked on one side, she pondered for quite a while before she'd risk her tiny 'tootsies' in the strange, rippling surf. Mind you, once she did venture into the warm, lively waters of this grand, new sandy world, there was no stopping her as she splashed about and both kids enjoyed a whale of a time splashing one another.

To the four of us, in deck chairs on the sand, the children's high spirited play was a comical joy to behold and a pleasant memory we'd always cherish. Chris, with her Brownie camera, jumped up to record these first happy shots of our two lovely youngsters on the beach. Only the sight of 'pop' bottles and food from the picnic basket lured the little rascals out of the sea. Covered in clinging, wet sand they plonked themselves down beside us while Madge wiped their hands with a towel, before they both happily tucked in to all the goodies.

Soon catching sight of nearby sand castles, the little imps were on their feet again engaged in feverish activity with tiny buckets and spades. John and I, boys at heart, were quickly pressed into service as moat makers and castle builders. With us on our hands and knees, sand flying everywhere, and the two kids chortling with delight, it was obviously a comical spectacle. Chris and Madge, still seated on their deck chairs, were killing themselves laughing at our antics and Chris shouted over, "When you four kids have finished that massive building project, are you," she collapsed laughing again, "are you going to fill the moat and raise the British Flag" she concluded, with a sarcastic chuckle. Still giggling, as Simon and Emily danced about with glee, Madge called, "You two'll never grow up, will you? Still, you're making a good job," she tittered, "and the kids've got a good pair of dads."

Chris was up again with her camera, "I've just got t'get a couple of shots of this for the album!" she cried, "Now, come on you lot, watch the 'birdie,' mam's goin' t'take your picture."

John and I struck an idiotic pose, while Emily and Simon held their buckets and spades aloft in giggling, happy triumph. "Marvellous!" cried Chris, "Just one more - hold still, now."

A couple of days later, before our promised visit to the afternoon Punch and Judy show, we all ambled along to nearby Llandudno Pier for a glorious whiff of sea breeze, a lovely view of the Great Orme's Head and the beautiful, imposing Bay of Llandudno. We still tease Emily about her amusing first visit. Walking along the Pier, for the very first time, Emily could see the swirling waters far below, between the wide gaps of the pier timbers. Suddenly seized by a strange fear that she might somehow slip through the cracks, she grabbed my hand and begged me to lift her up out of harm's way. Lifting and holding her close, her little face against my chest, I laughingly tried to reassure her. Arms around my neck, clinging tightly - her eyes closed, she stayed in my arms until we reached the pier end, where the timbers were closer and the cracks filled. Funnily enough, Emily was fine looking over the pier rail - it was just those awful cracks.

Pondering on poor little Emily's fears, my mind drifted back twelve or more years to when Pa had taken us, Kate and me, as kids, to the opening of the Mersey Tunnel. The day when, as we walked into that strange unknown environment, our Kate had grabbed my hand - just like Emily - and, with fear in her little blue eyes, whispered, " I'm a bit scared, Bernie, is it safe? D'you think the water might get in?"

Chris noticed my thoughtful look, as my mind wandered back from the past. "Penny?" she questioned, with a smile.

"Oh, was just thinking about our Kate. Wish she was home again, don't you?" I said sadly.

"Yeah, well, she qualifies this year y'know, and she might land an appointment nearer home." Chris answered, hopefully.

"I hope you're right, Chris, I do really. I miss her so much, at times." Tears filled my eyes, as I spoke.

"I know, luv, I know." Chris whispered, "I do too, y'know we all miss her, Bernie."

Emily tugging at Chris's skirt made us realise it would soon be time for Punch and Judy on the Prom. Kids don't give one much time for reflection, do they.

What we adults had to try and remember was that everything we saw today was a completely new experience for Emily and Simon. A Punch and Judy show, with its highly coloured, lifelike puppets, was something 'out of this world' for the children. Television characters of children's programmes hadn't yet reached Liverpool, and so the wild and wicked antics of Mr Punch, his wife, the policeman plus a string of sausages and, of course, the crocodile etc, were a source of great excitement and sheer delight. Shrieking with laughter, along with all the other kids, Emily and Simon were absolutely enthralled.

Lifting Emily up for a better view, it was hard to hold her as she wriggled and squirmed, waving her arms, shouting at Mr Punch when he belted someone with a stick and cheering madly when a brave soul got him back. We four parents were 'in stitches' at the antics of our offsprings, more than the capers of the puppets. I'd never seen Emily so excited, happy and delighted as she was that day on the Prom by the Pier. As can be imagined, we had to see the show quite a few times during our brief stay in Llandudno, but it was worth every second to see our 'imp's' faces.

Blue skies for most of the time meant that we really enjoyed the holiday, including a couple of trips on that wonderful Great Orme Tram. Simon and Emily were fascinated as the long car chugged its way laboriously up the steep slope, passing its partner on a loop line, on the way to the summit of Orme's Head. Alighting on the warm but breezy slopes of the mountain, we visited the kids play area and, of course, the little shop before enjoying our picnic lunch amidst glorious panoramic views surrounding us on all sides.

Enjoying their picnic in the heart of, never before visited, mountain scenery, the children's real thrills came from those wonderful tram rides up and down Llandudno's great mountain. Can't say I blame them really, big kid that I am. I love trams and puffers and I'll bet you do too.

Shortly after our holiday, we received the most important, long awaited, letter from Kate saying that she'd now qualified as a State Registered Nurse, having passed the senior State Examinations. Also she had the hospital certificate showing her qualifications and status as a trained nurse. For some considerable time, she'd gained great experience in the surgical ward and was now becoming a theatre Sister. It was a position she'd wanted since her early days in casualty.

Thrilled and delighted, we knew that our Kate was now really on her way in the worthwhile profession of her choice. I hoped and prayed that Kate would be able to secure a suitable position in Liverpool where I knew she, herself, wanted to be. My prayers were soon to be answered when Kate, early in 1948, delighted us all with the news that she was transferring to Liverpool's Smithdown Road General Hospital.

Now with little room available at our house, we had to find a place for Kate. After feverish activity and many enquiries, we managed to locate and secure a small flat for her in Elm Hall Drive. Quite nice, and handy for the hospital, it seemed ideal to me and Kate. She could always move later if it wasn't to her liking. At least she'd be home again, at last.

Kate's final home-coming was a very emotional affair. Despite her hardened attitude to life and the outer brittle shell nurses have to develop to shield their true feelings, Kate, at our first meeting after so long, just lost her well trained composure and wept. We all did, unashamedly.

With or without training, Kate was still very young; young enough to really miss her home, her family and all the friends she'd left behind for so long. Realisation that she wasn't going away again seemed to release over five years of pent up emotion. For a few fleeting moments, on that day when Kate came home, I saw before me the little girl who'd once gripped my hand tightly, years ago, to seek reassurance from her big brother. We'd never lost that strong bond of love between us. Deep down, we're all so very human.

Very pleased with the furnished flat, close to us at home, Kate settled in nicely. Also, she was delighted at the prospect of little Emily growing up and getting to know her as a real person, and not just an aunt from far away. Emily took the earliest opportunity to tell dear aunt Kate all about her first lovely holiday in Llandudno, including Punch and Judy's antics. Listening to the stories with bated breath and suitable astonishment, Kate delighted Emily with her patient, undivided attention.

For aunt and young niece, it was the first happy chance to really get acquainted and they both loved every minute. Loving children as she did, Kate looked upon Emily as the absolute 'apple of her eye.'

It was not long after Kate arrived back in Liverpool that, following a number of years separation, we met cousin Ruth once again. Mother's eldest sister's child, Ruth left home in her mid-teens and had, apparently, lived in and around the Blackpool area for some considerable time. Her mother's deteriorating health, after her father's death, had recently prompted her to return home.

As sometimes happens when families drift apart, we only chanced to meet up with our cousin again when her mother died. In a rather strained atmosphere of the funeral, we realised that Ruth, an only child and as yet unmarried, was not only, understandably, upset at her mother's death but seemingly very lonely as she had no local friends. This unexpected meeting with a young woman, remembered only in early life, was to have a strange effect upon our lives.

I remembered Ma, when Kate and I were growing up, mentioning that young cousin Ruth had left home and she wondered why. It was not a thing that kids in our families, at any rate, did in those days. Several years our senior, Ruth now looked very mature and even - if one might use the term - almost gaunt in appearance. Ma, with her usual friendly attitude, invited our long lost cousin to call round, whenever she fancied, for a meal and a chat. No need for her to be lonely now.

Over the following months, Ruth did visit us and Kate, when off duty, and she seemed quite friendly and happy to talk to the ladies but, I thought, a little sort of distant with Pa and me. Ruth appeared to regard my Ma, understandably I suppose, as a second mother. I was really pleased for her, of course, seeing that both her parents were now dead, but I always felt strangely uneasy in her presence.

Kate, now theatre Sister at the hospital, was fully occupied as were all the nurses and doctors in the surgical ward and other parts of a large busy hospital. Learning to understand and heal patients minds as well as their bodies, Kate, over six years training, came to realise that mental strain was reflected very much in behaviour. From her brief association with Ruth, Kate sensed a very disturbed state of mind in need of help. Ruth's underlying unhappiness seemed to be much more than just the recent death of her dear mother.

CHAPTER 8

Ruth

Over a week after Kate's conversation with me, Ruth called one evening in a very distressed state. Briefly greeting me in the hall she stood for several seconds near the kitchen door, her eyes reddened, almost in tears and looking very distraught. Ma jumped up from the table in alarm, "Whatever's the matter, luv," she asked, anxiously.

"Oh, I needed company, Auntie Bea, it's just I miss Mum so much, I wish to God I'd seen more of her these last years" Ruth blurted out, as she stood, trembling slightly, leaning against the dresser. Her eyes filled again and tears slowly trickled down her cheeks. Pulling out a chair, I put my arm round her waist to comfort and sit her down.

"Don't do that. Don't touch me," she almost spat out.And I felt her body stiffen. Shocked, I backed away peculiarly embarrassed, murmuring something like, "Oh, sorry Ruth, er, only trying to help". Chris looked at me strangely as Ma quickly intervened with, " Look, sit down, luv, and I'll get you a 'cuppa,' you'll feel better after a drop o'tea."

Little Emily, looking scared, whispered, "What's wrong Auntie Roof?"

"She's just a bit tired, luv, she's goin' to 'ave some tea." Ma answered, with strained cheerfulness. Emily moved shyly over and gently put her tiny hand on Ruth's knee, "You very tired, Auntie Roof? I'm tired sometimes, too." she murmured, with touching childish sympathy.

Ruth dried her eyes with a small pink hanky, "I 'spect y'do, luv." She tried to smile, looking at Emily with a curious mixture of affection and, to my mind, a deep, deep sadness. "We all get very tired sometimes, Emily, when things go wrong," she whispered, tearfully.

Ma brought in the tea and cake. "Just 'ave this for now, Ruth, and I'll make us all a nice meal later on."

"You're very kind, Auntie Bea," Ruth held back the tears, "just like Mom used to be," she whispered, shakily.

As Ma promised, we had a late meal and the evening passed quite amicably. About half nine, as Ruth said goodbye and turned to leave, she glanced briefly at me, blushed slightly, and whispered. "Cheerio, Bernie, sorry I snapped."

"Oh, well - that's okay - you were upset. Bye, Ruth." I said, rather automatically.

A moment later Ruth was at the door and Ma let her out. Chris turned to me, "Look. Bernie, I know she's upset about her mum an' that, but there's something odd about her - something I just can't fathom - I mean, that bit when you tried to sit her down, her eyes blazed, they really did."

"I know what you mean, Chris," I said, "but I think it's just nerves."

"She's lost both parents, feels a bit guilty at being away so long and she's been on her own a lot. She seems very jumpy. Kate and I were talking about this some time ago and Kate thinks she might be able to help Ruth calm down if something, other than her mother's death, is upsetting her."

"Feel very sorry for the gel, really," said Ma, sympathetically, "poor kid, wonder what she did in Blackpool?"

"P'raps she worked in a boarding house - there's plenty of them, aren't there?" Chris suggested.

During a week or two that followed, pressures of work and daily life soon dismissed Ruth from my thoughts until one day, I chanced to meet Kate on her way home from the hospital.

"Could you slip along tonight Bernie, there's something I'd like to discuss with you, on your own if pos?"

"Why, is anything wrong, Kate?" I asked, anxiously.

"Well, no, not exactly, it's about Ruth. I've had a word

and, well, I think it might be better if you're in the picture Bernie. Don't mention anything at home, you'll see why tonight."

A little apprehensive, I nervously told Chris that Kate needed some help in the new flat. In no way, really, was I prepared for Kate's - or rather - Ruth's revelations. In the forties, with no T.V. and newspaper reports far less explicit than today, we were much more easily shocked by strange and evil human frailties.

Although Ruth's lamentable story raised, in both of us, a sense of disgust, we felt, at the same time, a deep sympathy also for her as an innocent victim. But for the fact that she desperately needed an understanding confidante - near her own age - we might never have known of Ruth's bizarre unhappiness.

Already clear to me, Kate, a close relative, sympathetic and a trained nurse, must have also seemed to Ruth the obvious person in whom to confide. Her only real fractional bit of luck in years. Disclosing her burdensome secrets to someone who might help and not just deride her was, I'm sure, a great relief to a very distressed woman.

Having suffered an unhappy childhood, Ruth had, apparently, run away from home and ended up in - of all places - Blackpool. (That much we already knew.) There, she claimed, drifting into an unsuitable job and various other activities, had robbed her of the normal life she should have had. "Well, surely, Kate," I pointed out, "running away from home was her decision, why did she go?"

"For the same reason, I'm afraid," answered Kate, "that other poor kids try to escape."

"Escape?" I questioned.

"Yes, you see, she left Liverpool simply because - well, to put it bluntly, she was being molested."

"You mean - no - who by, for God's sake?" I exclaimed, incredulously.

Kate's demeanour was tense, "It just hasn't been easy for

her, Bernic, she'd had to endure sexual interference for a long time, poor girl." Kate's voice quivered with suppressed emotion.

"Why, in God's name, didn't she tell her mother and get it stopped," I cried.

Looking steadily at me, Kate said, firmly, "As you well know Bernie, I've been nursing for over six years now and during that time I've often seen the results of these perversions; they're more common than most people think," Kate hesitated briefly, "You see," she continued, "Ruth was sexually abused from a very early age Bernie, don't you understand?" Kate's eyes filled and she tried hard to stop the tears.

My totally shocked expression answered her question.

"Yes, Bernie," she murmured quietly, "it was her beastly father."

I was utterly stunned, I just couldn't take it in, I really couldn't. After several moments, I said, incredulously, "Are you sure, Kate, I mean, can she be telling the truth?"

Kate's expression hardened dramatically. "With respect Bernie, that's always the attitude of many people, particularly men. They don't, they can't believe the child involved." Kate's eyes blazed; I'd never seen her so angry. "Why should Ruth lie now?" she cried, " her rotten father's dead. The bastard's ruined her life. He warped her thinking in the really formative years, the pig."

Kate, frightfully distressed, remained silent trying to regain her normal composure.

"I hardly know what to say, Kate, but I'm heartily sorry," I said quietly, breaking the silence. "It's so hard for me to understand such behaviour from a father. I mean, did her mother know?" I felt awkward asking the question.

Kate, now once again the dispassionate nurse, answered coldly, "That's where these animals are so crafty, so cunning, they cover their tracks and always seem normal. From Ruth's early age, he played the loving father in such a way that her little mind believed their relationship was normal. To tell mummy though would make her jealous. It must be their little secret. The dirty rotten pig. So, to a degree," Kate continued, bitterly, "he poisoned her small mind against her mother. It was quite some time, at school, before she began to realise her father's duplicity and started to partly blame herself for what happened between them."

Eventually, despite cajolery and veiled threats from her father, Ruth told her mother. This move only resulted in more harm than good. So plausible were her father's explanations and denials that her mother didn't - or didn't want to - believe her. As one can imagine, the atmosphere became so explosive and intolerable that she left home with few belongings and very little money.

"Good God! Where'd she go?" I exclaimed, "Poor kid could've come to us, couldn't she? She must have been very young, where did she live on her own at that age?"

"That, I've only just discovered." Kate said, sadly. "You see, Bernie, I've only given you an outline of the story from her first disclosures. Being very upset, mainly because of falling out with her mother, Ruth only told me the rest of her sad yarn yesterday evening. I had to let her tell me very slowly, in her own good time. It was a heartrending and very painful process, Bernie, I can tell you!"

"I believe you, Kate. It seems a blessing that you're here to help her. Did she manage to patch things up with her mother before she died?"

"Yes, well, she did, but although her mother had come to realise that she'd been telling the truth and the rift between them had been healed, Ruth felt that they'd lost so many precious years together and, now her dear mother is dead, she can't regain the love and affection she really needs."

'Yeah, Kate, I know, she said as much at home, a week ago. She seemed very distraught and that's when she nearly 'bit' my 'ead off for touching her. Maybe, now, I can see why, Kate."

"No, Bernie, I don't think you can, really. There's so much more to it than that. Something which worries her most of all and which she could never bring herself to tell her dying mother. Conscience is a very difficult thing to cope with at times Bernie. Ruth just had to share her burden with someone and I probably seemed the one member of the family who might understand."

"Well, Kate, at this juncture, I'm sure she was right to do so, but did she contact her mother when she left home? I mean, the woman must've been worried sick even if they had fallen out."

"Oh, yes, but the note she left her mum, concerning her whereabouts, was purposely vague in case her father saw it and found or pestered her," replied Kate.

"Well, obviously," I smiled sadly, "she'd planned her escape and had secured a refuge."

"Yes, indeed," Kate smiled for the first time, "she'd got 'in tow' with a girl friend - a bit of a 'fly-by-night' hussy, as it turned out - who's aunt ran a boarding house in Blackpool. That's how and why they both ended up there working for their keep."

"Well, that couldn't 'ave been too bad she might'ave done worse," I observed, lightly.

"Possibly; at the outset, maybe," continued Kate, "but Ruth's life, under her older friend's influence, didn't exactly continue in that relatively innocent vein. Y'see Bernie, Blackpool, as you know, is a bustling holiday resort and a large boarding house catered for many temporary visitors intent on pleasure and entertainment of all and every kind throughout the year."

"What you're really saying is that she got involved in the less savoury side of the holiday scene," I interrupted.

"Well, my dear, the thing is, many unattached males staying in the town had plenty of money to burn and Joan, Ruth's friend, 'tarted herself up' and wasted no time in presenting herself to well spoken, moneyed clients as an 'evening escort'! On a strictly cash basis, of course. As always, in this life, money - and plenty of it - was a great temptation to young girls.

Ruth, resisting at first, was eventually enticed by Joan's glowing accounts of her escapades and wads of lovely bank notes waved under her nose. The really sad, unfortunate thing was that Ruth, aware that she'd already been raped by her father, felt, mistakenly of course, that receiving money from a rich client for a service she'd already performed 'for free,' wasn't all that bad!"

"You really mean she actually got involved in this sordid activity?" I exclaimed, "I can't believe it, one of our family."

"Yes, I'm afraid so," Kate said sadly, "but as she now realises, she was becoming involved in a dangerous, soul destroying 'profession'. Ruth was literally jumping into a pool of iniquity at the deep end. Quick, easy money, a curious sense of power gained over some clients whom she came to regard as either weak or stupid and a distorted sense of glamour, drove her ever further into the mire.

Although carefully selecting clients - for various reasons - she found herself becoming insensitive, hard and callous with an ultimate feeling of revulsion and disgust for anything sexual and a total dislike of men and their attitude towards women.

A pattern so familiar to many ladies of the night who, sooner or later, come to realise that this dubious, 'oldest of professions' is rather like a scorpion with, more often than not, a frightful sting in the tail."

"I must say, Kate," I murmured, gloomily, "you paint a vivid, disturbing and, no doubt, truthful picture of Ruth's drift into - well, I find it hard to say - prostitution. It really distresses me to think that 'our cousin' should get involved in this whole sordid business. I mean, the revolting incidents with her father - well, I might understand that, but this - I can't imagine how she could consider such a step - it disgusts me, Kate, it really does."

"Me too, Bernie, to a degree, but she's so regretful and bitterly unhappy that I feel so very sorry for her. Y'see, what I've told you is, perhaps, only half the story." Kate hesitated again, preparing for her final revelations, no doubt anticipating my reaction.

"To put it briefly, Bernie, the last straw was when a jealous client attacked her. Ruth broke down when she described how this bastard attacked her with a knife. Fighting him off, she managed to 'club him' with a heavy table lamp, and, God knows how, she survived."

"Good God, the swine, that's terrible, no wonder she's a bag of nerves," I gasped.

Kate, her hands trembling slightly, continued, "Thing is, Bernie, he's marked her. She's got a scar on her neck and shoulder, I've seen it. I wish she'd killed the sod. Some men are just animals."

For quite a while, Kate was silent and obviously seething within. She was consumed with anger and desperately sorry for our unfortunate cousin, and so was I.

"There's one thing that really gets to me, Bernie," Kate eventually whispered, very emotionally. "Y'see, Ruth, poor kid, gave birth to a stillborn child, just over two years ago. Oh, God. she needs our help, Bernie, she really does."

Kate's last few words quivered with heartfelt emotion and again, she was very close to tears.

A lump came to my throat as I tried to come to terms with innumerable emotions which seemed to flit through my mind. A vivid picture of Ruth's tragic life passed before me and I felt nothing but compassion and a great thankfulness for my own life.

Some time later, in a calmer frame of mind, Kate and I agreed that the family couldn't yet be told and all the disclosures would remain absolutely confidential. Ruth had had enough worry and grief, she now needed a little real help and affection, for a change. It must be left to Ruth, herself, as to whether or not she wished to tell Ma or Chris anything about her unhappy past. What *their* reaction would be to the full story, I dreaded to think.

Chris and I, so far, had no secrets from each other and my knowledge of Ruth's story had, I felt, put me in a very difficult situation. It might become a mental balancing act, I could well do without, trying to avoid letting anything slip in conversation. With young Emily growing up in normal conditions and, I hope, having a normal happy life, Chris might be upset if she discovered I'd known all about Ruth's past and kept quiet. It could lead to needless unpleasantness. I could only hope that past history would remain buried, and I'd try to forget the unhappy saga.

My sombre mood, concerning Ruth, wasn't really lightened when I met her, a couple of days later, in Smithdown Road where she'd got a temporary job in a sweetshop.

Desperately trying to hold a normal conversation with Ruth, whilst endeavouring to avoid revealing my inner thoughts, I did notice that she seemed a bit brighter and more at ease; possibly because she'd now shared her dark secret with our Kate. As we parted, however, and I watched her slowly walking away towards the shop where she worked, I suddenly felt that earlier sadness and anger at the thought of her father's revolting behaviour towards her during her early years. That man, that animal had helped to ruin her young life. If he hadn't killed her physically, he'd nearly destroyed her mentally and pushed her into that shocking life in Blackpool.

Gloomily turning to go home, Ruth still in my thoughts, I somehow felt strangely guilty and almost ashamed to be a man. An alien idea that frightened me and a thing which had never before crossed my mind. For a moment, little Emily's presence, her wonderful trust and the love she had for me, filled my thoughts and heart with a new joy which lightened my hitherto dismal mood.

Thinking of my beautiful small daughter, I wondered how any man could betray that loving trust or defile that perfect innocence. It was just quite beyond my comprehension. Walking back along Smithdown Road, on that late summer afternoon, I noticed two little girls - about Emily's age - playing with their dolls on a doorstep. Passing the carefree pair, I inwardly prayed for their future safety and happiness and I felt reluctant tears trickling down my cheeks, there in the street as I made my way home to my happy normal family. I, we, had a great deal to be thankful for.

CHAPTER 9

Onwards towards the Fifties

With a bit of money saved from job overtime and extra, sideline wireless work, I mentioned the idea, to Chris, of buying a small, secondhand car. When she'd 'descended from the ceiling,' so to speak, I calmed her down with the news that our good neighbour who worked in the paint trade, intended buying a new vehicle and was prepared to sell the old one at a reasonable price.

As I pointed out, "The car's in good 'nick' and would be great for us, with Emily growing up and everything. If we find it too expensive, well, we could always sell it."

"Who to," came the quick, sarcastic response from Chris. As my dad once said, "Our women have a happy knack of putting the 'mockers' on a good thing, particularly if money's involved." Anyway, to cut a long story short, our neighbour did let us have the 'dream on wheels,' in the autumn, for a down payment with an agreement to pay the balance in Spring of 1949. We were really in business. Snag was, I couldn't drive.

Now driving schools weren't 'hanging off every tree' in the forties, and, even if they were, I couldn't afford the fees or time, anyway. So, I taught myself. Oh, a friendly mechanic came with me once or twice, he must have had nerves of steel but, by and large, I managed alone.

As those learning to drive will appreciate, holding the wheel and sorting out the pedals on a car for the first time, can be a very daunting experience. Sitting in the driving seat, at my first attempt, the space surrounding me in that little car seemed, to my eyes, like the inside of a bus. My thoughts at that moment were, 'My God! Am I in charge of this.' With three pedals to consider, I wished, like the three legged dancer, that I'd got three feet.

I must admit that I 'sorted out' the gears a time or two before I really got the knack. It's a wonder that the gear wheels weren't worn smooth. With wild-eyed disbelief, Chris said, very wisely, "I'll wait till y'get the hang of it before I take a trip."

Pa laughed till the tears rolled down his cheeks as he watched the car's 'hop-along-cassidy's,' progress up and down our vacant street, with its L plates flapping and 'jungle juice' in the petrol tank. Fortunately, mine was the only car in the stree, very few people had one. As Pa tittered, so eloquently. "And a bloody good job, too."

Apart from the fact that initial co-ordination of eyes, hands and feet is nerve rackingly difficult, one could so easily knock some poor old lady 'for six,' as she started to cross the road! What really worried me more was that I might do the same thing when she was still on the pavement. However, joking apart, I did manage to master my shortcomings and become a reasonably safe and competent driver. Much to the relief and delight of all the family.

Our little Emily's excitement when 'goin' in the big mota' and her complete, innocent confidence in 'daddy' as a driver, was a source of great amusement to Ma and Pa. Occasional runs through Gateacre to Tarbock, Cronton and district, were trips into grassy, leafy wilds at this time but now, I suppose, this area is built up and well populated.

I soon found that obtaining a licence and passing a test were only the first steps in car ownership. Routine maintenance was something I had to learn to save money. However, good condition, a fairly simple, accessible engine and associated parts, seemed to present little cause for alarm to even a novice like myself. Washing and polishing our 'little beauty's' bodywork was a chore with which both Pa and Chris lent a hand.

Chris rapidly became 'car minded' and, to my alarm, (and many other husbands since) announced her desire to learn driving. As most married men know, trying to dissuade a woman when her mind's made up is like swimming in treacle.

Came the day when I had to instruct my dear wife in the art of controlling - hardly driving - a motor car. With pounding heart and secret misgivings, I sat beside her in the passenger seat. Having already briefed her with relevant diagrams, I proceeded to put theory into practice.

"Hand brake on, gear lever in neutral, check mirror, pull out choke." I whispered, and then, with great trepidation, "Start the engine." Sound of the engine coming to life hadn't, until now, altered my blood pressure one jot, but this time, well, one can imagine.

"Check mirror, activate indicator, now press the clutch pedal down with your left foot, darling. No, no, that's the brake. That's it - now gear lever to left and into first. NO, don't let the pedal up, release handbrake, check mirror and now slowly release clutch, while gently pressing right pedal." OOPS! BANG! Engine stalled. Poor Chris's knuckles were white as she tightly gripped the steering wheel. A look of dismay crossed her pretty face. "Relax." I muttered, I should talk.

"Try again, but this time both pedals nice an' easy together. As one comes up the other goes down, nice an' steady."

This time, Chris got it more or less and we slowly, jerkily moved forward. "The road's moving," she gasped.

"No, now take it easy, *we* are" I tried to reassure. We drifted the full length of the street, in first gear, before shuddering to a shaky halt as I told her to brake and disengage the clutch.

Several nerve shattering sessions later, Chris had mastered changing gear, while still keeping her eye on the road. She was beginning to gain confidence. As in my case, when I started, it seemed a good job that all forward car gears were synchro-

CHRIS LEARNS TO DRIVE - 1948!
D'YOU VERY MUCH MIND, DARLIN'!
STONE THE RUDDY CROWS!
HOW'M I DOIN'-LUV?
DON'T ASK!
GOD! SHE'S ROUGH ON THEM GEARS!
1-MAY-2
L
OH, NO!
V.L. EDWARDS.
CHRIS PRAYS TO PASS THE TEST: I JUST PRAY TO GOD!
(NOTE-FORTIES 'HILLMAN MINX')

mesh. Our little Hillman Minx took quite a pounding in the early days.

One day, unbeknown to Chris and just before one of her last learning jaunts, I sponged the car unholstery with a special cleaner. Setting off, with the windows down, she didn't seem to notice the 'pong' but later, in a layby, I could see her sniffing. "What's that funny smell," she murmured, "is there something wrong? Can y'smell it?" This was too much for my perverted sense of humour.

"Smell it Chris, dearie, blimey, charlie, I'm sitting in it." I guffawed, looking her straight in the eye. "Dirty devil you. I'm not that bad at driving." Giggling, she hit me in feigned annoyance.

We both burst out laughing and little Emily, sitting on a special seat I'd made for her behind Chris clapped hands and laughed with us, although she didn't see the joke.

"What daddy say?" she giggled.

"Oh," answered Chris, "he's just tryin' to be funny, sez y'mom can't drive very well."

"You dwive good, Mom. Daddy ony funnin, Mom," Emily cried, gleefully, looking a bit reproachfully at me.

"Course she does," I grinned, "Just funnin', Emily. She's the best mom in the world, isn't she?"

"Yes, best mom in the world," Emily shouted, clapping her tiny hands and then blowing her mom a big kiss.

"Thanks luv," Chris's eyes filled and she leaned over the front seat to kiss Emily. "At least I've got one admirer." Chris chortled, settling back in her seat.

I turned and kissed her cheek, "Oh, I think you might have a couple," I whispered, finding her hand and squeezing it gently.

Today would be memorable for its warm summer sunshine, pleasant picnic and the fact that Chris was soon to take her final car test. We'd have two competent drivers in the family which would prove to be an invaluable asset in our future lives.

A couple of days after our trip, Chris took and passed her test and, a few weeks later, Kate passed the exam in our little car after a lot of diligent practise. Kate is a perfectionist in everything she tackles. She'll soon have a car of her own, I'm very sure of that.

Although the strain of teaching - best I could - Chris and Kate to drive was something I hadn't anticipated, the effort turned out to be well worthwhile. It meant that the car was used and looked after when I was at work. Ma, Pa and Chris's mum got out much more often and so, I'm glad to say, did poor Ruth. Her health and outlook greatly improved during the time she was back home with part of a happy family she'd missed so much. Even Ruth's physical appearance changed and her facial features softened. A bit of real affection does really work wonders. Her unhappy story tended to drift to the back of my mind - as it obviously had in hers - where, I felt, it would gradually fade and cease to be a threat to anyone's future. It just had to be forgotten.

Having a car was a great advantage for trips to Wales and other places but time was a limiting factor in my case. Work was priority number one to build up our savings and pay the ever present bills. When Emily was a little older, Chris might, she thought, return to hairdressing - part time - to help achieve our future ambitions - Bernie's pipe dreams - as Chris called them. Anyway, we'd managed one, the car.

Seeing Emily growing up and having the car, we liked to take 'snaps' occasionally and this got us interested in the rapidly, developing craze of amateur cinematography. Reading library books on the subject and studying '*Amateur Cine World*,' we picked out a second-hand 9.5mm cine camera from an advert. With this camera, it would be possible to record Emily's antics - and ours - for posterity. The 'Dekko' camera secured, we now needed a projector. To save expense, I bought a hand operated 'Pathescope Kid' projector to which I fitted a speed controlled motor.

The motor came from electrical stock, while the drive pulley and belt was 'Meccano.' A real 'Heath Robinson.' Very good equipment in 8mm, 9.5mm and, of course, the semi-professional 16mm film, was available but we had to be satisfied with what we had for the time being.

Due to its centrally placed perforations, 9.5 film had a picture nearly the size of the 16mm type and so we, with our little 9.5 Dekko camera, managed to capture some really good family shots.

Emily was 'tickled pink' performing for the camera and loved being a movie star like her favourite, Myrna Loy. The one great drawback of cine film was the fact that any mistakes, bad focus, incorrect exposure or camera shake etc, couldn't be corrected. What one shot was what one got. Modern video can be 'wiped' and re-shot immediately - we had no such luxury. Still, with a bit of care, we enjoyed ourselves and got some quite passable results.

The great thing about our little projector was that it would 'throw' a three by two foot picture onto a screen quite easily! Much larger than the average T.V. set. Comical holiday movies weren't the only source of entertainment - in the absence of television - for 'Pathescope Ltd' produced a wide range of professionally made 9.5 films for sale and hire. Drama, comedy, cartoons and many more types of film were available on 30, 60, 200 and 300ft reels to suit every taste and wallet.

Emily constantly worried us to buy cartoons and 'funnies' which she'd watch again and again, until the poor old projector was red hot. Chortling with glee, she'd follow the antics of Donald Duck, Betty Boop and Mickey Mouse and shout for more when the films finished. That was the one snag, someone had to be there to change reels and keep our Emily happy. Pa was often the 'projectionist' pressed into service and, I'm afraid, our film struck daughter had dear old Pa a trifle 'moth eaten' at times.

When I was available - which wasn't very often - Emily would sit on my knee to watch the filmed adventures of Charlie Chaplin, Laurel and Hardy or even George Formby while Chris and I laughed heartily at our kid's pleasure and excitement, rather than the film. Emily Shirley was a happy, intelligent and wonderful daughter. I suppose every parent thinks that about their offspring. You must forgive me. She was growing up fast and, in no time at all, our little girl would soon be going to school. The thought made me realise that this year was the last of a decade. New Year would herald the start of the fifties. I couldn't help wondering what the next ten years would bring - especially for all of *us*.

I hoped and prayed that fate would smile on our child and enable her to achieve a better life and standard of living. Before and during the War, times had been very difficult for us and we were determined to provide opportunities for Emily which were sadly lacking in our young lives.

Creation of the Welfare State, in 1948, seemed to be a governmental step in the right direction, which might bring a substantial improvement to our lives. Everyone really hoped so.

Kate seemed very contented in her profession and was convinced that her future career prospects were good in the newly developing National Health Service. Dedication, care and understanding of folk's needs would make Kate - S.R.N. - a valued member of any community.

While, maybe, slightly biased in favour of my sister's capabilities, I really believe that all nurses deserve more recognition than they now receive, and a much increased remuneration.

Kate's understanding friendship with Ruth, since she returned home, has certainly helped to restore that very disturbed girl's self respect. I feel extremely glad that Ruth has begun to 'fit in' with us as a normal family and to lose some of her 'hang-ups.' Over the last few months, strange as it seems, Kate and I have never again mentioned Ruth's unhappy disclosures. I think we both realise that it's better to let unpleasant, sleeping ghosts lie! We both just try to help quietly, without words. Ruth, too, without any reminders will need a long period of normality before fully recovering from her Blackpool memories and childhood ordeal.

Late summer and early autumn were quite pleasant and Chris, who was able to use the car far more than Kate or me, was becoming a very proficient driver. Emily seeing her mum driving was probably a good thing for she was growing up in an environment soon to be dominated by the motor car. Surrounded too by rapidly developing technology in the form of aircraft, the radio and television industry and cinematography, she could quickly learn to become a "Thoroughly Modern Millie.'

Great technical advances will be made in Emily's lifetime and I only hope that society's attitudes will improve at the same rate, to make her world a better place in which to live. Principal factors for the future must surely be people's outlook and their ability to care for the environment and to use the new, exciting technology wisely.

Obviously, sophisticated games were not around for Emily's fourth birthday, last August, but still she was spoiled by everyone, with lots of other gifts which pleased a four year old - many more presents than we ever received as kids. Although thrilled to bits with various toys and games, the real joy of Emily's special day was the large, waking, sleeping, well dressed doll from Chris and me. A constant companion, even in bed 'Dolly' was talked to, cuddled, dressed and undressed and, of course, often needed new clothes. Another job for hard worked mum.

One day, when the three of us were lolling on a grassy bank in Greenbank Park, I gazed at Emily clutching the ever present doll and, smiling at Chris, I laughingly exploded, "D'you know, our Emily, that flippin' doll's better dressed than we are."

Looking proudly at her little friend's fancy outfit and then, a trifle reproachfully, up at me, Emily's expression changed and she giggled, "Daddy's jealous mom, cos Dolly looks nice."

Chris and I took a fit of laughing. "You're dead right, girlie," I tittered, " I feel like a tramp beside 'er. Can't you just make me a new suit, Chris?" I joked.

Both girls laughing heartily, Chris said, "Your dad'll have to get a lot more money, won't he, Emily? That's if he wants a new suit."

"S'pect so," Emily's grin slowly faded and then, with head slighted tilted and a sad little thoughtful look, she asked, "Will daddy want lots an' lots of money for a new suit?" She looked so very sad. For a moment, a lump came to my throat as I gazed at her disturbed little eyes staring up at me. Young as she was, she worried about me and the pennies. Quickly, I leaned forward and put my arms around her and Dolly. "Don't you worry your pretty little 'ead, luv," I grinned, "your mom's only 'funnin!' I'm not that hard up yet, I'll get a new suit next year, maybe, our Emily."

Playfully tousling her hair, I kissed Emily's forehead and stroked Dolly's chin. Happy and giggling, she snuggled closer with Dolly and, looking up, she whispered, "We both luv you, daddy."

"I know, luv," I murmured, squeezing her tightly and kissing her cheek. Those few innocent words, from my lovely small daughter, meant so much more to me than any material possessions could ever hope to do. Chris, with joyful tears in her eyes, smiled at us and blew a kiss. At that moment in time, on a sunny afternoon in Greenbank Park, we were, indeed, three - maybe four - very happy people.

As usual, time just seemed to fly and Christmas, the last of the forties was upon us. With less food shortages and a little more money to spend, the whole family enjoyed the festivities far more than in many previous years. Our prospects were very slowly improving. For a change, new glittering decorations and bits of tinsel adorned the walls and ceiling of our small home, while a lovely Christmas tree, embellished with innumerable silver bells and shining baubles, stood majestically, in the parlour corner.

'Up with the lark,' on Chrismas morning, Emily, bright eyed and excited, nipped into the parlour knowing she'd find the gifts, from Father Christmas, beneath that wonderful, sparkling tree.

Despite having to spend a short time up at the garden nursery, early on Chrismas day, I got back by early afternoon and it didn't spoil our enjoyment. Everything prepared, we all sat down to a hearty, festive meal at a table groaning under the strain of the usual Xmas fare, including a very large and appetizing turkey. This was a real treat to us when we thought back to wartime shortages.

Coloured trinkets and Christmas crackers bedecked the table and the familiar 'corny' gags were, I'm afraid, read out after the meal, from the many cracker mottoes. Gurgling with delight, Emily displayed a 'diamond' ring found in a cracker. Proudly, she slipped the glittering prize onto her tiny finger and held it aloft for all to see, "Just like Mom's," she exclaimed, joyfully.

"Oh, it's great, Emily." I cried and added with a smirk, "and the very same price as your mom's."

Chris belted me and chortled, "I might've guessed, you. I always thought it came from Woolies."

"I did warn you, Chris," her mother laughed.

"Never mind, Chris," I whispered, leaning across and patting her hand, "next year's our sugar wedding, so I'll buy you a nice of lump of sugar."

Laughter all round followed this remark and Chris tittered, "Oh, will y'now. That'll be nice. What the heck's a sugar wedding anyhow, when it's at 'ome?"

"Well, it's six years, isn't it?" I replied, "When you've been married six years, it's a sugar and candy wedding and," I added, with gentle sarcasm, "you're really so very sweet, my poppet. Isn't that right Emily, your mom's sweet?"

Emily giggled gleefully, raising her right hand high and pointing comically at Chris, she murmured shyly, "Mom's great."

"Flattery won't get you two anywhere," Chris laughed, as Emily ran across and buried her head in her mom's lap. Everyone laughed and applauded when Chris lifted our blushing offspring onto her knee and cuddled her. Kate, sitting next to Chris, leaned forward to tickle Emily under the chin and then kissed her cheek.

Emily's podgy little hand shot up to stroke Kate's face and she pursed her lips in a kiss. "Luv you, too. Auntie Kate." she whispered, sheepishly. Our Kate's smile broadened as she gently squeezed her niece's hand and kissed her again.

My sisters deep affection for our small girl meant so much to us and we were absolutely delighted that Kate was back home with the family this Christmas and New Year, after such a long absence. I felt happy, too, that her presence here, in Liverpool, had been so fortunate for poor Ruth. With Kate's friendship and sensitive support, I could see Ruth carving out a brand new life for herself, with a brighter future she really deserved. Here, at the party, Ruth certainly seemed less tense and was, like the rest of us, looking forward to the start of the fifties, a new decade, a trip into uncharted, but calmer waters, I hope.

As a State Registered Nurse and, at the moment, a theatre Sister, our Kate's career was really taking off and I'm sure that, with her drive and ability, she'll reach the top. Since she came back home, Kate and I seemed to have rekindled that old spark of very close affection; the curious bond we always had as kids. As mi dad often often used to say, "those kids are like two peas in a pod,"

Although still working in horticulture bills must be paid and a bit of wireless business, my interest in the new television could be invaluable when it becomes common-place in Liverpool. (Holme Moss, opening on October 12th 1951, would transmit T.V. to our area)

Photography, as I've said, was Kate's hobby but I also dabbled in the art and not always appreciated by the rest of the household - I developed and printed photos in a blacked out bathroom.

Because technology was developing so rapidly in every sphere, I just felt that I had to be part of it. Chris didn't really mind because she was interested as well. Time always seemed to be the enemy though, there were never enough hours in the day.

Sometimes I felt rather sorry for Chris, as I do for many a mum, because being a mum cramped her style a bit. She had so much talent it seemed a shame to waste. First class at professional hairdressing, she was also good in horticulture and, of course, needlework. Chris could drive, skate, beat me at mathematics and was a damn good manager. She'd always had to be. I hope she doesn't read this or she'll never get her hat on. Oh, there's just one thing I forgot to mention, she's a great mum too, I know Emily agrees with that.

Even if she hasn't reached her full potential, Chris always wanted to be Emily's mum and nothing could ever change that desire. She always dreamed of her own lovely, little 'Shirley Temple' and she wasn't disappointed.

Over the years, both our parents have been marvellous. Unfortunately, Chris's dad died comparatively young but her mam, young brother and uncle were always there for us in good times and bad. Our dad and ma have been a tower of strength to Kate and me during some very difficult days and our present wellbeing is proof of their care and deep affection for us as we grew up.

Looking back, I often wonder just how they managed in the early days and how we all survived so well. Christmastime now seems a lifetime away from those in the twenty-thirty period and, as the last few days of 1949 slip away, I hope that we and old Liverpool will never ever return to the terrible deprivation of twenty or thirty years ago.

As prospects improve for us and we're able to acquire more of life's little luxuries, we teach Emily to value what she has and, most importantly, the value of money and that it doesn't 'grow on trees'. Young as she is, I think she's getting the message and will grow up as 'canny' as her mum.

Emily, like the rest of us, looked forward to this New Year because I'd told her it was a bit special, being last of the decade. Just as at Christmas, all the family was gathered together, in our house, for the joyful celebration. With food a plenty, whisky and wine on hand and the Christmas decorations still giving the place an air of festivity, we all thoroughly enjoyed the evening listening to wireless music and waiting for the final midnight chimes of Big Ben from London, to usher in the year of 1950.

Visibly tired, yet quite lively, Emily was really 'tickled pink' at the idea of staying up way beyond her normal bedtime to see daddy let in the Great New Year, at midnight. With everyone busy listening to the lively wireless music, I slipped out around five minutes to twelve - suitably dressed - into the freezing cold night air. Feverishly checking my watch by torchlight, I awaited the precise moment to ring the doorbell. Midnight. Church bells rang out - maroons and hooters blared and even firework rockets illuminated the darkened sky. As if by magic, when I pressed the bell, the front door flew open to the frenzied shouts of, "Happy New Year, Bernie." "Happy New Year, Daddy!" In Chris's arms, excited Emily grabbed me for a first kiss as Chris hugged me close and kissed me too. Surging forward, everyone voiced their frantic greetings, with handshakes, hugs and kisses all round. With a pandemonium of laughter, merriment and shouts of, "Happy New Year. Welcome to 1950. Good Luck for the Fifties," and what have you, the year of 1950 was well and truly ushered in, while Big Ben, on the wireless, hammered out twelve booming chimes to herald in the Great New Year. The start of 1950 and a brand new decade. Auld Lang Syne and spirited, lively strains of Scottish music filled the room as we all raised our glasses to toast the New Year. As I watched our Emily, with both tiny hands clasping her glass, draining the last drops of fizzy lemonade, my mind flitted back and forth over the past, present and way, way into the future. For a fleeting moment, my heart felt slightly heavy and I worried for Emily's tomorrow, much as Ma and Pa must have done for Kate and me, in days gone by.

Suddenly, I felt curiously elated and, quickly raising my glass for a second time, I cried, "Friends, Good Luck to you all. Never let's dwell on the bad bits of the past or what might happen in the future. Let's remember the good times, there were lots of them - and the great folks who helped us when we were down. Let's drink to a brighter tomorrow, for all of us. I give you a toast, everyone, to a great and wonderful 1950 and beyond. All the Very Best."

Everybody cheered and applauded, above the lively music on the wireless, and drained their glasses. "Very good, Son, great," laughed my dad, "couldn't 'ave put it better miself, 'Ere 'ave a refill," he grinned, filling my glass.

Tipsy conversation and laughter continued well into the small hours before we all eventually retired, in rather disorderly fashion, on camp beds and settees as well as more normal quarters.

Fortunately, our vivacious small daughter was persuaded to slip between the sheets of her own little bed, just before one o'clock. She didn't need much persuasion, I can tell you.

New Years Day was a lazy time for most of the family, but Kate was needed at the hospital and I had to spend some time at the garden nursery. With only a skeleton staff, over the holiday, to check the greenhouses and boilers, I was on my own for much of the time. It was during this quieter period, alone, that I began to reflect on the past and to consider the future, the possible time we all had ahead of us.

1950 could be the start of a whole new way of life for us as a family. At twenty seven, my adult life had begun to prosper and little Emily would attend school for the very first time. Chris might return to hairdressing - part time - to boost the household budget, while Ma and Pa or Chris's mum would spend more time keeping an eye on young Emily. I was very much hoping to become involved in the developing television business, along with radio, as wireless was now called.

Kate, I'd no doubt, would make great strides in the, much needed, nursing profession and Ruth, despite her setbacks, was moving forward to a new life with admirable resolution. The new decade would, I was sure, present novel ideas and create fresh opportunities for Chris, myself and Kate, beyond our present aspirations.

Over those past twenty-seven years, about which I've written, life had been comparatively slow and leisurely, but the times ahead should prove to be much more exciting and dynamic. They do say that it's an ill wind that blows no good to anyone and, from the boost given to technology by the developments made in the War, this appears to be true. The speed of life was rapidly changing, I hoped that the quality did the same.

Emily was growing up in, I hoped, a brave new world. We were all cautiously optimistic about the prospects in the fifties and sixties. At this point in time we, in Liverpool as elsewhere, were awakening to the new technological revolution. Oh, I know that we, as a family, hadn't yet moved into the new era, but we were getting there. Up to 1950, we hadn't become famous or hit the headlines, we hadn't yet produced a marvellous invention and Kate hadn't yet married an earl. In fact, I suppose, we hadn't done anything very spectacular, except to be ourselves and try very hard to make the grade. But, d'you know something, I think that, in our own small way, we were really beginning to do just that. We three (working class) kids from old Liverpool.

We intended to keep trying.

THE END (of the beginning.)